'Well, thank for forgivin grin took a out of the w

'You can return the favour some night, if you like,' Jo answered, this time without the necessary pause for thought. Eeahh! She'd sounded as if she was angling for an invitation. Worse. A date.

He frowned and said vaguely, 'Yeah, that would be nice. Very nice.'

She didn't believe him, and was a little shocked at how much she suddenly minded that he thought of her so totally as a colleague. Not really a whole person. Definitely not a woman.

She opened the door and he stepped past her before she had it quite wide enough. He brushed close, and even though they didn't touch, and their eyes didn't meet, there was something...

Lilian Darcy is Australian, but has strong ties to the USA through her American husband. They have four growing children, and currently live in Canberra, Australia. Lilian has written over forty romance novels, and still has more story ideas crowding into her head than she knows what to do with. Her work has appeared on romance bestseller lists, and two of her plays have been nominated for major Australian writing awards. 'I'll keep writing as long as people keep reading my books,' she says. 'It's all I've ever wanted to do, and I love it.'

Recent titles by the same author:

THE DOCTORS' FIRE RESCUE
CARING FOR HIS BABIES
THE A&E CONSULTANT'S SECRET*
THE DOCTOR'S UNEXPECTED FAMILY*
THE HONOURABLE MIDWIFE*
THE MIDWIFE'S COURAGE*
THE SURGEON'S PROPOSAL

**Glenfallon, an Australian Country Hospital* mini-series

THE LIFE SAVER

BY
LILIAN DARCY

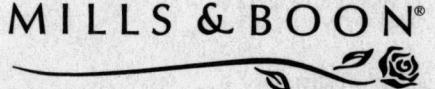

DID YOU PURCHASE THIS BOOK WITHOUT A COVER?

If you did, you should be aware it is **stolen property** as it was reported *unsold and destroyed* by a retailer. Neither the author nor the publisher has received any payment for this book.

All the characters in this book have no existence outside the imagination of the author, and have no relation whatsoever to anyone bearing the same name or names. They are not even distantly inspired by any individual known or unknown to the author, and all the incidents are pure invention.

All Rights Reserved including the right of reproduction in whole or in part in any form. This edition is published by arrangement with Harlequin Enterprises II B.V. The text of this publication or any part thereof may not be reproduced or transmitted in any form or by any means, electronic or mechanical, including photocopying, recording, storage in an information retrieval system, or otherwise, without the written permission of the publisher.

This book is sold subject to the condition that it shall not, by way of trade or otherwise, be lent, resold, hired out or otherwise circulated without the prior consent of the publisher in any form of binding or cover other than that in which it is published and without a similar condition including this condition being imposed on the subsequent purchaser.

MILLS & BOON and MILLS & BOON with the Rose Device are registered trademarks of the publisher.

First published in Great Britain 2005
Harlequin Mills & Boon Limited,
Eton House, 18-24 Paradise Road, Richmond, Surrey TW9 1SR

© Lilian Darcy 2005

ISBN 0 263 84347 5

Set in Times Roman 10½ on 12 pt.
03-1205-49445

Printed and bound in Spain
by Litografia Rosés, S.A., Barcelona

CHAPTER ONE

WHEN Dr Ripley Taylor observed seventy-six-year-old Thornton Liddle commence his lumbering journey from the side door of the new pharmacy to his beat-up old pick-up truck parked in back of the Harriet Professional Building, then pause beneath a still bare-branched maple tree for the stealthy lighting of a cigarette, he reflected on how difficult it was for even a grown man to smoke in secret without getting caught out.

Sure, you could sneak around to the back of a building, shrink the window of potential discovery down to bare minimum by puffing like crazy four times a minute, and even hide the offending cigarette behind your back when you were sprung, but the little ribbon of blue smoke rising just beyond your shoulder still gave you away.

Assuming the interloper's eyesight was good enough, of course.

'Doc...' said Thornton Liddle, his rheumy eyes crinkling in a smile.

He sounded cheerful, and more hale and hearty than any man of his age had any right to be, given his diet, habits and lifestyle. He'd come in with a chest infection that morning, and Rip had prescribed antibiotics, which Mr Liddle confidently expected to restore him to full health by the time he made a follow-up visit in a week or so. The medication would probably do exactly that, too. It really wasn't fair.

'Didn't see you there,' the elderly man went on. 'You should be standing in our nice Vermont spring sunshine, not huddled over there in the cold. Take a whiff of that air! Blowing in all sorts of fresh ideas. Happens with the change of season. Myself, I was just thinking I'd like to... um...'

He stopped, realised what he had in his hand, gave a guilty grin, dropped it on the ground with only the first half-inch turned to ash, and ground it out beneath his heel.

'Just taking a couple of puffs,' he promised, as eager to please as a little boy. 'Working on stopping. Wife won't give up going on at me over it. Says I'm on my last carton, or else. Honest, and I know she's right, because I've read the information leaflets, and I see the TV commercials.'

'That's good, Mr Liddle,' Ripley said. 'A good effort. I know it's hard when you've been a forty-a-day man for fifty years.'

Now, please, get in the car, because I think my fingers are about to start burning.

He held his breath.

'Better be getting home,' the old man said.

'Yes, and give Mona my best, won't you?'

Both husband and wife had been Rip's patients for more than six years, since he'd joined the two-doctor Harriet Family Medicine Center, Duchesne County, Vermont, as the junior family practice specialist. He was the senior partner in the practice, now.

'Will do,' Thornton agreed.

'See you soon, Mr Liddle.'

Hot ash fell into Rip's palm and he dropped his burned-down cigarette in time to lift a hand and wave at Thornton, who had climbed into his pick-up and coaxed the old engine into life. Rip didn't dare use his foot to snuff out the final curl of smoke emanating from the butt, because it was such a tell-tale movement, and any second now Thornton would wheel his vehicle around in the direction of the parking lot exit and Rip, his foot and his cigarette would be in the old man's direct line of sight.

The big, unwieldy vehicle made an inefficient turn, one tyre bumping the circle of concrete that protected the base of a shade-giving tree. Thornton headed for the road a little too fast, then came to an abrupt halt as another car went by just as he was about to zoom out into the far lane. No more cars coming. The vehicle jerked forward again.

Ah, at last Mr Liddle had gone, and Rip was safe.

Safe from discovery, replenished with nicotine, and totally disgusted with himself.

Of all his patients, he would least have chosen to be almost sprung by Thornton Liddle, who didn't need his doctor to be setting a bad example in the lifestyle department, and who really couldn't defy the odds on a smoker's health risks for much longer. His chest infections were getting more frequent, and he was taking blood-pressure medication and a strong diuretic. He was significantly overweight, and congestive heart failure had become a likely scenario.

Some people might argue that, at seventy-six, Thornton Liddle had earned the right to slowly kill himself any way he chose, but Rip happened to know that his pension would cut out at his death, leaving his wife, aged a healthy sixty-seven, with an income on which she couldn't survive, and a cool-headed daughter-in-law who'd already announced that she didn't have spare room, time or money enough to give her husband's mother a home.

If Mr Liddle's eyes hadn't been almost as bad as his clogged-up chest—with his sight and reaction times the way they were, he shouldn't still be driving, but that was a different issue—the old man would have caught his family doctor out in a flagrant case of the pot calling the kettle black.

Actually, *disgusted* didn't begin to encompass how Rip felt.

His scalp tingled, his chest felt tight, his heart was as heavy as a stone. He didn't want to be this person—the kind of doctor who couldn't take his own advice, and the kind of man who kept on picking over the past and punishing himself for something that, rationally, wasn't by any means all his own fault and anyhow was over and done with now, because he had the signed and sealed divorce papers to prove it.

His next patient was undoubtedly waiting. He'd been gone too long already. He'd tried unsuccessfully twice last year to stop smoking. 'And that, Ripley Edward Taylor, was your very last cigarette,' he muttered.

This was exactly what he'd said to himself eight years ago, at age twenty-eight, when Tara had convinced him to give up, and for seven years after that—until his and Tara's divorce last year—he'd succeeded in avoiding the evil stuff. That first time, however, he'd given up for love, which was surely a much more powerful motivation than…than…

What was motivating him now?

Oh, yes. That's right. Guilt.

More than guilt, he thought, but couldn't put a finger on his reasons right at the moment.

Spring?

Mr Liddle had talked about changes in the air, coming with the change of season.

Maybe there was something sound in the theory.

Rip took the offending, wonderfully aromatic packet out of his back pocket, and didn't have to count to know that there were still about fifteen cigarettes left in it. He could tell by the weight. Fighting the deluded conviction that it was a terrible waste of good tobacco, he tossed the packet into the open dumpster behind the Harriet Café, slipped in through the back door of the professional building and waited for the withdrawal symptoms to kick in.

'You are in a foul mood, Ripley,' his junior partner Dr Josephine Middleton told him at a quarter to seven that evening.

'No, I'm not,' he answered, but he knew she was right.

He wasn't going to tell Jo yet that he'd given up smoking. He didn't want to give her any ammunition. Not when she looked as if she herself could travel the distance between here and a foul mood in about a minute and a half. He'd read something like that on a T-shirt once, only it had been phrased more succinctly, thanks to the use of a five-letter B-word rhyming with 'witch' that he would never apply to Jo Middleton, even at his and her mutual worst.

'I'm not going to argue,' she said.

'Which *is* an argument, Jo, because the subtext is sticking out a mile.'

'Can we get on with this?'

'With what?'

'With our discussion on whether we're going to switch pathology labs.'

'I thought we'd decided to hang fire for a couple more months, keep a closer eye on their statistics and make a more informed assessment then.'

'That's what you suggested. It's not a decision.'

'So you don't agree?'

'There have been two results lately that I'd have expected an immediate phone call about, not just a written report in the mail, and the lab's waiting times on some of its cytology tests have blown out by a week or more in the past year, I'd say.'

'You've done the figures on that?'

'No, I'm going with my gut feeling, and I think we should vote with our feet.'

'Sorry, but I don't work that way.' Ripley stood up, fighting with himself not to open the second drawer of his desk, where, going with his own gut feeling, he was pretty confident he might find a crumpled cigarette packet with a couple still left in it.

'So we're locking up? We're done?' She sounded very impatient.

He sat down again. He had a headache, and realised that every muscle in his face was tight. He should have gone up to Stowe for some spring skiing on the weekend. Jo had been on call, so he'd been free. Translation—without an excuse. And yet he hadn't gone, the way he hadn't gone on several other occasions over the winter, even though he knew it did him good to get out there on the mountain, speed beneath his feet and cold air in his lungs.

The sense of disappointment in himself didn't improve his mood.

He let out a rasp of breath. 'No, OK, we need to at least make a decision on when and how we're going to make a decision, don't we?'

'If you're going to start talking like a politician, we should definitely leave this until tomorrow.'

'No, you wanted something now, let's get to something now.' He felt stubborn suddenly, at sea as to what she really wanted, irritated up to his aching eyeballs.

He liked Jo enormously. She was the kind of practice partner he could utterly rely on. She matched him in her capacity for work, her attention to detail and her willingness to wash out her own coffee-cup. She even cleaned the microwave occasionally. Ninety-five per cent of the time, they got on so well that he didn't have to think about her, and that had really helped over the past eighteen months when all he'd been able to think about in any spare moment had been the divorce.

Why hadn't he seen it coming? Why hadn't his commitment to their marriage been enough? Why couldn't Tara have talked about what had been wrong earlier, so they might have had a chance at fixing it? And what the hell had she seen in Trent Serrano? The man had to be a symptom of the problem, surely, and not its cause. Therefore, what should Rip himself have done differently?

'OK,' Jo said. 'I'm giving this five more minutes.'

Because it was ten to seven, and if she didn't get out of here in five minutes, she'd miss the start of…

What day was it?

Tuesday.

What show was it vitally important for her not to miss on Tuesdays at seven?

She couldn't remember, but she knew there was one, because she'd debated setting her DVD to record it before she'd left the house that morning, but had decided it wasn't necessary since by seven she'd definitely be home.

Only at this rate, she wouldn't be.

And dealing with Ripley Taylor in one of the worst moods she'd seen him in for a long time did not count as an appealing alternative. Normally, she would have found one of their rare disagreements stimulating. He was good to argue with, because he always kept his sense of humour. Today, however…

If he thought she hadn't noticed he was trying to give up smoking again, boy, was he kidding himself!

'Get some figures down on paper, Jo,' he said. 'Tell me I'm pulling rank if you like, but I'm really not going to switch labs without some cold, hard stats in front of me. I'm a scientist. I'm not a damned crystal ball gazing, intuitive…' he cast an absent-minded, irritable look in her direction—specifically, at her hair, which to be honest wasn't in its best ever mood either—then finished, '...witch.'

'Right. OK. Stats,' she said, while thinking, *Witch?*

Ripley didn't look all that spectacular himself, if she studied him closely and decided to be unmerciful about it.

There were some silver threads in his dark hair, and some deepening lines around his eyes and mouth. His skin had a natural light olive tone, but he didn't spend enough time out of doors—or hadn't lately, anyhow—so you'd hardly detect it, and especially not in the fluorescent light of his office. He looked washed out. Even his strong shoulders looked a little less square than they used to, and his cognac brown eyes were tired.

She felt a momentary pang of concern for him, and then her anger came back. He was holding her up, he was about as charming as a bull at a rodeo, he'd just called her a witch without even realizing it apparently, and still somehow she felt *tender* towards him? Just how much of a pushover was she prepared to be here?

No, thank you!

It was six minutes to seven.

'Then and only then we'll talk again, all right, Jo?' he said, his tone clipped. 'Now, if there's nothing else...?'

As if she had been the one who'd held him back with a circular discussion, not the other way around, when she really, really did not want to miss...whatever her show was.

'There's nothing else,' she said, and was out the front door, still fuming about that word 'witch' before it even occurred to her that she'd just left Ripley to lock up without so much as an 'Is it OK if I leave you to lock up?'

He'd routinely been the last one to head for home almost every night since Tara had left him so Jo had taken his locking up for granted, but that was no excuse. She sighed, thought about going back in, actually paused on her way towards the car, then remembered the 'witch' line and the start of her Tuesday show, and left him to it.

Got home with seconds to spare.

Raced in the door.

Switched on some lights.

Almost tripped over the cat.

Grabbed the TV guide, tore a page while flicking through it, found the day and the time, found the show, which she'd highlighted at the beginning of the week in pink highlighter pen…

Oh.

Her current third favourite crime show, with that tell-tale little 'R' in the listing that showed it was a repeat. She hadn't noticed that, either the other day while highlighting or this morning while trying to decide whether to record.

Her heart sank, and she muttered to the printed page, 'Excuse me? Are we not in a ratings period right now?' But she turned the TV on anyhow.

Miffy miaowed and rubbed her sleek black side against Jo's leg. She was hungry and wanted her dinner.

So did Jo.

Eggs on toast suggested themselves as the most likely option, the way they suggested themselves at least twice a week. The other nights she usually messed around with some pre-packaged meal that she would sometimes attempt to improve by, say, adding mushrooms. Mostly, it didn't work. When her grandmother Mamie had been alive, Jo had cooked a lot more—cooked for real and with pleasure, instead of messing around, because Mamie had enjoyed her food and had given lots of compliments on Jo's cooking—but it didn't make sense to do that after a long day when you were only cooking for one.

She gave Miffy her dinner, then wandered back into the

little entrance hall to dump her purse on the hall table. She caught sight of herself in the mirror, and the first word that sprang into her mind, sadly, was exactly the one that Rip had used.

Witch.

She shouldn't be angry with him.

He was right.

She did look like a witch.

A relatively young and robust witch, true, at thirty-four, but with all the hallmarks of serious archetypal witchiness latent in her appearance...and in her lifestyle. Eccentric spinster living alone with a black cat, talking to herself, fixated on a personal calendar marked by television shows instead of the more traditional lunar cycle, and prone to making experimental potions involving mushrooms and frozen TV dinners in the kitchen.

'Josephine,' she told the mirror, 'you are in a rut.' She stared at her reflection for several minutes, as the full truth of this statement struck home.

Oh, lord, was she ever in a rut!

She'd known it somewhere in her heart, but she hadn't *seen* it. She'd stubbornly insisted to herself that her life was smooth and safe and that she was content. She had an older sister in Connecticut whom she spoke with every week on the phone and saw several times a year. She had active, happy parents, who had a serious travel addiction, on top of her father's business basing him in places like Singapore and Tokyo for extensive stretches. Mom and Dad brought her interesting stories and souvenirs from all corners of the globe at regular intervals, and this old house of Mamie's would be a veritable treasure trove soon. She had a satisfying career, with co-workers she both trusted and liked.

All the same, it wasn't enough, and she was in a rut.

It had begun through no fault of her own three and a

half years ago when dear Mamie had had her first stroke, while Mom and Dad had still been in Singapore. By the time Mamie had died eighteen months later, aged eighty-five, Jo had been pretty strung out—emotionally and physically exhausted, really—after taking care of her as well as holding down a demanding professional job, and the rut had gotten deeper.

She'd probably needed the rut then. For a while. Even when she'd first arrived in Vermont to join the practice and live with her grandmother, she'd probably still been dragging some baggage from the awful break-up with Jack in their final year of family practice residency. Even if you only looked at Mamie's death as the cause, however, two years had gone by now.

The hair was only a symptom, but what a symptom! She was way overdue for a trim, so she'd been scraping it back into a ponytail lately, but the ponytail was too bushy, and sometimes a strand would catch and pull so she'd pull the elastic out without even thinking about it.

She must have done that at some point that afternoon, and her hair streamed and rippled from the crown of her head to her shoulders, which could be a good look on some people but not when it was this, um, this...

'Wild,' she tried, out loud.

Be honest at least, Jo.

Tangled.

Dragged through a bush backwards.

Witchy.

And the colour seemed dull, somehow, as if even her hair was telling her that she needed to get a life. Natural redheads needed shine, and if they didn't have shine, they needed something to camouflage the fact that they didn't have shine.

I can't cook eggs on toast tonight.

I can't watch TV.

Restless, irritable and unhappy, she went into the kitchen, found some wine under the sink and stuck it in the freezer to chill more quickly. The five cartons of ice cream greeted her like old friends when she opened the freezer door, and like old friends they were each different, each with their own unique appeal.

Tonight she chose chocolate-chip cookie dough. Three scoops. Waffle cone, because a bowl and a spoon would be far too staid. Changed into snug-fitting navy stretch sweats and a grey knit cotton top, but resisted the thick violet-and-yellow bedsocks. Bedsocks were part of the rut.

To be honest, ice cream was part of the rut also, but, like Rip with his new, not-yet-admitted-to campaign to quit smoking, Jo knew that she had to take things one step at a time. Ice cream held a special place in her heart, and not just because the stuff had to be Vermont's best-known export.

And I have to fix more than just my hair.

I have to fix my life.

But the hair was a start.

She grabbed the telephone directory that covered this part of Vermont. She'd never managed monogamy when it came to hairdressers, and knew from previous flips through the relevant listing that there were a couple around here who would come to your home. Maybe even after seven at night, if it was a real emergency.

OK, here. Hayley's Hair at Home.

Hayley was a honey. She responded like an ambulance on full lights and sirens, and correctly diagnosed the problem at once. Jo needed a new look the way a drug dealer with multiple gunshot wounds—not that Jo saw many of those in Harriet—needed a transfusion.

'We are going to cut, we are going to condition and we are going to bleach,' Hayley decreed.

'Bleach?' Jo had never considered that.

'Just highlights.'

'On a redhead?'

'Trust me. That peachy autumn leaf shade, with sun-kissed strands on top. You are so-o-o lucky to have this hair. It will look fabulous.'

Two hours and a second glass of wine later, Jo agreed. 'I *love* it!'

And I think I've reached the point in my life where I'm ready to settle down and try for hairdresser monogamy after all…

Hayley departed in a bouncy mood—she'd had a glass of wine, too—but she must have forgotten something in her mobile miracle hairdressing kit because five minutes later the doorbell sounded once more.

CHAPTER TWO

NINE twenty-five on a Tuesday night.

Was that too late, Rip wondered two seconds after he'd pressed the bell.

He and Jo were both doctors. He wouldn't have hesitated, wouldn't even have thought about it if this had been a medical emergency, but it was…no, not quite personal, but close. He was there to apologise for being so sore-headed earlier in the evening in his office.

It was a professional visit really, he decided, but he and Jo had always stayed so completely out of each other's personal lives, scrupulous to a fault on the issue, that simply coming to her house felt like stepping over a line. In five years he'd only been there a handful of times, almost always in daylight, never for more than a brief visit, very much focused on work.

Walking up the herringbone brick path that led to the front steps, he'd noted how cosy and pretty Jo had the house looking now. When she'd first moved in with Mamie—the whole town had called Jo's grandmother Mamie—the place had been a little run down. Bare patches in the front lawn, some straggling shrubs, bland paint colours on the clapboard and trim, nothing but dust and an old porch swing to welcome a visitor when they reached the top of the steps.

Now the lawn was all filled in, if still brownish after its most recent covering of snow just a few days ago. There were spring bulbs poking up green fingers all through the flower-beds that ran along in front of the porch, and café-style chairs and a round table already sitting on the wide porch floorboards ready for the warmer weather.

And Jo had painted the place herself.

When? Last year?

He vaguely remembered her talking about it. It had probably been one of those thoughtful, gentle attempts of hers to get him to think about something other than medicine or the divorce, and he probably hadn't been grateful enough for it at the time. She'd used three different colours that no doubt had silly names on the paint-sample brochures but were really a golden cream, a grey-green and a rusty brownish, darkish red. Reddish.

OK, maybe you did need the silly colour names, he decided as he waited for Jo to answer the door.

He heard her footsteps, the rattle of the knob and a creak as she flung the door wide. 'Did you forg—? Oh.' Her face changed. 'Rip.'

'I came to apologise.' Maybe she wouldn't even ask him in. 'For earlier, in the office.'

'That's OK. I put it down to the nicotine withdrawal.'

'How did you know I'd—' He stopped and re-thought. 'I guess that's how you knew. Because I was in such a foul mood.'

'I'm perceptive that way.' She smiled. 'But don't stand there on the doorstep. Come in.'

She seemed serious about the invitation, so he did.

The place was comfortably untidy. She'd flung her jacket over the back of a chair earlier, and there were two empty mugs on the coffee-table, along with some magazines and a TV guide folded back to today's page. He glimpsed pink highlighting on the listings in several places.

The room smelled strange. Astringent, like bleach. He looked at Jo, dressed down in her sweats. She looked very comfortable. He realised she'd done something to her hair and mentioned the fact in exactly that phrasing.

'You've done something to your hair.'

'Try that again, Ripley.' She grinned at him. 'You're supposed to say, "Wow, your hair looks fabulous, what have you done to it?"'

'No, I'm not,' he shot back at her. 'I'm male. I'm supposed to say something obtuse and vaguely accusatory, as if you've confused me unfairly with such a change and I might be in danger of not recognising you any more. And that's exactly what I did say.'

She laughed.

Thank goodness.

'And now, as a female, am I supposed to explain the finer points of a cut and style, conditioning treatment and highlights until your eyes glaze over?'

'Something like that. And my eyes will glaze over. But it does look good.'

'Thanks.' So he could see the full effect, she did a little pirouette, which surprised them both. She wasn't a very demonstrative, physical person. Didn't flirt. Never showed off.

Ripley appreciated the change to how she looked in the same untutored way he'd appreciated the paint colours. Her hair was shorter and shinier and lighter on top, bouncier and a much better shape. It made her head look elegant, showed off a perfect profile he'd never noticed before, and revealed a graceful neck that he'd never noticed before either.

But the real change was in how pleased she seemed about it. He'd never thought of her as bubbly, but she seemed bubbly tonight. Bubbli*er*.

'I've been thinking,' they both said at the same time.

'You go first,' Jo told him. 'Shall I make us coffee? I

had two glasses of wine tonight and— Oh!' She frowned. 'I'm starving. Have you eaten? Shall I make us omelettes?'

'Omelettes and coffee?'

'Omelettes and whatever. Coffee and whatever.' She waved a hand.

'An omelette and one of those glasses of wine for me, if there's some left.'

'There is. I opened a bottle. There's plenty left. I really only had two glasses. Hayley had one, too.'

Hayley?

'The make-over emergency worker,' she explained. 'Hairdresser to you.'

'Right. That's why you're bubbly? Potent combination of hair and wine?'

'Am I bubbly?'

'Yes.'

'No, it's not really the wine. It's partly the hair. And I think I'm going to put away my TV for a while, I've decided. I think I'm in a rut.'

'That's what you've been thinking about?'

'No... Well, not until tonight. No, I've been thinking about the practice. I think our load is too heavy and we need a third partner.'

Which was exactly what Rip had been thinking. Either that, or close their books on new patients and send them elsewhere—to the newer practice in Netherby with which they shared the after-hours on-call roster. But for some reason the third partner idea appealed more. Some fresh blood, a fresh perspective. Their patient load had increased so gradually that they'd gotten overworked without realising it, and to be honest he'd welcomed the long hours over the past year—the late finishes, the Saturday appointments, the more frequent call-outs, the evening sessions on Mondays.

But Tara had gone. He had to accept it. You could be

one hundred per cent committed to the idea of marriage yourself, but if the other person wasn't, your own commitment couldn't sway the result. Their divorce had been made final nearly ten months ago and it was time to move on, throw open a few windows, not bury himself ever deeper in work.

It seemed auspicious that he and Jo had both had the same idea about how to handle the situation. He stood in the kitchen watching her make the omelettes—mushroom and cheese—and they talked about it in more detail, with only the most trivial of disagreements about a couple of points.

Their shared vision reminded him of how bad-tempered he'd been earlier in the evening—so bad-tempered, especially when she'd left him to lock up the practice, that he hadn't even considered apologising to her about it until after nine, by which time he'd had a peanut-butter sandwich, thrown away a couple more packets of cigarettes, been for a two-mile run, waxed his skis and sharpened their edges, and taken a long shower. The ends of his hair were still damp.

'I really am sorry about earlier,' he said.

'About calling me a witch?'

'*That?* That's what got to you the most? I have no idea why I even said it!'

She shrugged and grinned, sheepish this time, and touched her straw-and-beech-leaf hair. 'Don't you see the connection? Witch? Emergency after-hours hair makeover?'

'I didn't realise you cared that much about my opinion.'

'Of course I care about your opinion!' She wheeled around and put her hands on her hips, huffy and indignant but mocking her own spirited reaction at the same time. 'We work together every day. I respect you. I like you.

You often do it, you know. You say something, and it takes me by surprise so I don't react on the spot, then I go home and think about it and decide that you're right.'

'So I'm a deeply influential figure in your life.'

She laughed again, and didn't answer, and he couldn't think of the right thing to say next either, so they were both silent for a good two or three minutes. She put bread in the toaster, deftly folded the first omelette in half, flipped it onto a plate, buttered and triangled the toast, poured the second batch of lightly beaten egg into the pan and added the sautéed mushrooms and a sprinkling of grated cheese.

He watched her, appreciating the way she moved, and the way she didn't bother to look at him, which gave him free rein to continue looking at her.

She was utterly different from Tara. That was his first conclusion.

Tara was tiny and nimble and fiery, like Tinkerbell in *Peter Pan*. She had fair skin with cheeks that flushed to a hot rose when she was happy or angry or hard at work. She had dark hair and big dark eyes that could flash at you with a dozen different emotions in the space of a few hours.

For years Rip had been captivated and fascinated by the rapid shifts in her moods, by the emotion and energy and talent she put into her singing and her work with fabric, by her saucy selfishness and her moments of extravagant generosity. From when he'd first known her, she'd had a trust fund from her grandfather's estate which had given her a large enough income to live on and a corresponding attitude of flexibility and insouciance, and he knew that was part of the appeal. She had the luxury of being a free spirit, and he hadn't met too many of those.

He'd probably still be captivated if she was still around, but he'd started to accept that she wouldn't ever be.

Physically, Jo was much larger. Big-boned? Full-figured?

No, because those were so often euphemisms for 'overweight' and she definitely wasn't that. But she was strong, smooth-skinned, smooth in her movements. Like the curving branches of a sycamore tree, or something. Her colouring was far less exotic than Tara's. It was the coloring of Vermont itself. The fall tones of her hair, her pale skin like the winter snow, her green eyes like river water running over moss.

And emotionally…

Calm, steady, reliable. The kind of woman whose generosity and perception you didn't notice for a good while because she was always so quiet about it.

The kind of woman whom you took for granted and didn't appreciate until it was too late?

A jab of apprehension suddenly stuck him in the chest like a blunt knife. Was there a subtext to her suggestion of taking on a third partner? Was it a prelude to her easing her way out and moving on? She'd come to Harriet mainly for her grandmother's sake, since her parents were out of the country so much, and Mamie had been gone for almost two years now.

'There!' With her usual easy, unhurried smile, Jo slid a filled plate towards him, complete with a sprig of parsley as a garnish.

'Thanks,' he said. 'It looks great.'

'Where do you want to sit? Dining table or couch?'

'I'm not fussy.'

'Dining table,' she decided. 'Since I'm giving up TV.'

'Is it as addictive as smoking, then?'

'Oh…' She laughed and shrugged, leading the way through the kitchen door to the small dining room where the table only seated four. 'Less addictive, I guess. But just as bad for my health right now.'

'Why is that?' He sat down, absently watched her topping up his wine and lighting two candles, even though she didn't turn the electric lighting down low. Why had she done that?

'Because I really am in a rut,' she said, sitting opposite him. She played with the softening candle wax for a moment, as if she'd lit the flames purely to have something to fiddle with. Her fingers were long and fine, with nicely shaped oval nails, covered in a clear polish. 'It's time to make some changes.'

Oh, hell, she really is going to leave, he thought. How can I get her to change her mind? What can I find for her in Harriet to keep her here?

His mind flipped through an insane set of options. Bigger house. Better office. Their nicest, least troublesome patients. A free season ski pass at Stowe. A blind date with one of the local ice-cream millionaires.

He wanted to tell her, 'Don't!' but she hadn't said it in so many words and he didn't want to put ideas into her head, or bring the issue to crisis point if she was still only mulling over her future plans.

What did she need?

Why wasn't she happy here?

Gosh, he didn't know her at all!

Hiding a panic he didn't understand, Rip put his heart and soul into at least making some appropriate conversation, and after they'd covered how delicious the omelettes were and whether this was a wine he'd tried before, he actually managed to ask something sensible and fairly discreetly worded about where she saw herself in five years' time.

She laughed. 'In Paris, floating in a boat down the River Seine.' She gave a fake double-take. 'Oh, we're not talking about my vacation plans?'

'You can,' he invited her, then added more honestly, 'But I wasn't.'

'I have some great vacation plans.'

She shouldn't torture him like this.

'But if you're asking about my professional plans, and my life plans...' She stopped and looked at him across the candle flames as he took a large gulp of his wine. Her eyes had gone a little smoky, grey more than green. The flames reflected in them as points of golden light, and light hit her new hair from above also, showing off its pretty shape again. 'I guess I'll be here.' She spoke slowly. 'Unless there's a reason to leave.'

He had to ask, 'There isn't one at the moment?'

'No. I don't think so.'

Damn! He *had* put the idea into her head.

'I don't want there to be a reason to leave,' she added. 'No, on balance, Rip, I think you can pretty much count on me staying in Harriet.'

And the blazing rush of relief he felt on hearing that statement from her set off a ripple effect which threw him off course for the rest of the evening.

CHAPTER THREE

'BOY, that nicotine withdrawal is really hitting you hard, Rip, isn't it?' Jo said to her colleague at the door, an hour and twenty minutes after she'd first put his omelette on a plate.

'Does it show that much?'

'You seem, oh, off-line somehow. Inhabiting a slightly different universe.'

He gave a vague smile. 'Sorry.'

'It's fine. Way better than the bear-with-a-sore-head routine you were pulling earlier, I have to say.'

'Right.' His jaw went even more square than usual, its strength emphasised by the day's growth of beard shadow. 'Thanks for the feedback.'

'Oops. I'm making the bear come back.'

'No, you're not, I'm sorry, I—'

'It's OK, Ripley,' she told him gently, tempted to touch him on the arm. In the end, she didn't.

Was he coming down with something, though, on top of giving up smoking?

She felt a wash of concern. He was always so competent. Back when he and Tara had looked like a happy couple—from the outside, at least—he had clearly been the one who had held all the practical stuff together. Jo had often heard him phoning his wife during a break between patients to remind her about some household detail, a bill to pay or an errand to run.

Tara was flaky. Fun and fascinating and highly creative, but definitely flaky. Jo could see the attraction to the male eye, but was glad she didn't have the requisite testosterone levels that made a man so vulnerable in that area. Tara would be very high maintenance, in every sense of the phrase. She had needed someone solid and strong and clever and perceptive like Rip, who was up to the task.

And even after the separation, when he had clearly been racked, his competence had only increased. To the point, actually, where Jo had had some professional concern that he might be headed for a breakdown.

Was that still a risk?

She considered telling him not to give up the cigarettes yet, that maybe he needed them for a bit longer.

But she knew that his smoking had always been a weakness he'd despised in himself, so she didn't speak. He'd taken it up at the invincible, all-knowing age of sixteen, and even medical school hadn't scared him away from the vice.

Tara had succeeded where an internship rotation through the oncology unit had failed. She'd told him that passively inhaling the smoke killed her singing voice, which had been a legitimate concern, given her ambitions in that area.

'Well, thanks for feeding me, and for forgiving me,' Rip said. His grin took any cloying humility out of the words.

'You can return the favour some night, if you like,' Jo answered, this time without the necessary pause for thought. Eeahh! She'd sounded as if she was angling for an invitation. Worse. A date.

He frowned and said vaguely, 'Yeah, that would be nice. Very nice.'

She didn't believe him, and was a little shocked at how much she suddenly minded that he thought of her so totally as a colleague. Not really a whole person. Definitely not a female.

Which was ridiculous, because on that front she'd always felt just the same about him.

Good to work with.

Very married.

And then very *not,* and therefore even more thoroughly off Jo's hormonal radar screen. Not that he'd ever looked hang-dog about it, but he'd been so rigidly encased in his shock and pain for the past, oh, eighteen months or more, no woman could have misread the vibes he gave off.

'Mmm,' she answered, as if she was already thinking about something else, even though she wasn't.

She opened the door and he stepped past her before she had it quite wide enough. He brushed close, and even though they didn't touch and their eyes didn't meet, there was something…

It was her imagination.

Nothing else.

'We'll talk about that new partner some more tomorrow, yes?' he said. 'Run it past Trudy and Dotty, see what they say?'

'Yes, we should.' The two women shared the job of practice manager, overlapping some of their hours and working others separately, and they'd both been at the helm for years. 'Goodnight, then, Rip.'

'Yeah, see you tomorrow. Thanks again. I…uh…yeah.'

He turned back to her slightly, in the middle of the porch, shrugging, smiling and frowning all at the same time, poor, helpless, nicotine-deprived man.

'Get a patch,' she told him.

'A what?'

'A nicotine patch.'

'No, but I will have you over to dinner,' he answered, his tone resolute.

Nicotine patch. Jo to dinner.

'Someone tell me the connection, Miffy,' she said to her cat thirty seconds later, with the door safely shut behind her, 'Because I can't spot it.'

Rip usually gave himself a couple of patient-free hours on a Wednesday morning, and so did Jo. He'd wasted numerous such hours in the months after Tara's dramatic departure. The blurred print of a single page of a medical journal would sit in front of him for an hour at a time while his thoughts churned and his staff wrongly believed he was locked in concentration.

Lately, he'd been doing a lot better—actually reading when he intended to, getting interested, retaining the information, applying it to patients in his practice, picking up the phone to call a colleague without a feeling of dread in case he got asked some well-meaning question that reminded him of the failure of his marriage.

Today, he went onto the internet and hunted up any recent detail on nicotine-replacement treatments. It was information he'd glibly recited to some of his patients in the past, but it felt different to think about applying it to himself. He took his own blood pressure, ran through the list of side effects possible when using a patch. The drug company was obligated to list such side effects, and so they should be, but there was a downside—the power of the human imagination.

So the symptoms of an accidental overdose of nicotine associated with the use of the patch could include confusion, cold sweats and drooling? On top of the daunting prospect of doing without the familiar ritual of a cigarette, was it surprising if some smokers looked at that list of possibilities, imagined them all happening at once, and lost their taste for quitting?

As the scientific literature and the anecdotal evidence

suggested, the nicotine patch was only effective if you really wanted to stop. You had to do the work yourself, you couldn't expect the nicotine replacement treatment to do it for you.

He kept hearing Jo's advice in his head. 'Get a patch.'

In other words, 'Don't dump your bad mood on the rest of us for the next however many weeks.'

Last night he'd said an instinctive no, but now he wondered if the advice was right. He didn't want to be unfair to her. She'd said she wasn't planning to leave, but if there was something that could tip the scales for her in that direction it could easily be her professional relationship with him. If that screamed downhill due to the symptoms of his nicotine withdrawal…

OK. He was motivated. He was a doctor. And he really didn't want Jo to leave. He'd try it.

Since he had samples in his drawer, he rolled up his sleeve and put one on right away, choosing the twenty-one-milligram size since he'd been smoking slightly more than a pack a day. As the instructions suggested, the patch itched and tingled on his skin for a while. About twenty minutes, which wasn't too bad. He'd seen patients with more sensitive skin have stronger reactions than that.

Last night he'd also said he would invite Jo to dinner very soon, but for some reason he felt obliged to put that one in the Too Hard basket for the moment. It wasn't as if he lacked opportunities to ask her after all. If one didn't come today, it would tomorrow. He saw her—glimpsed her, smiled at her, exchanged a few words—several times a day, five days a week.

And today they were having a meeting over lunch, after he'd seen a short morning's worth of patients between ten and noon. Running a little late, he ushered the last one out at twelve-fifteen and invited Trudy, Dotty and Jo in, as well as Practice Nurse Merril Heath and billing clerk Amanda.

'Are you safe to be around today?' Jo murmured to him as she passed, bringing her own chair.

'I'm wearing a patch,' he murmured back.

'Oh, I thought you said no to that idea last night.'

'Changed my mind.'

She nodded in approval, and he thought to himself that they shared a secret now.

As secrets went, it wasn't that earth-shattering or scandalous. If anyone asked, he'd happily tell. But at the meeting no one did ask, and he caught a little twinkle in Jo's eyes occasionally, suggesting that they were conspirators because she knew exactly what an ugly bear he'd been last night, and exactly what was putting him in a much more presentable mood right now.

That morning, she'd done what he'd asked and had collated some figures on the deterioration in service from their pathology lab that she'd perceived over the past few months. The figures confirmed her intuition and he felt bad, not because he'd asked for the figures, as he really did want some concrete evidence, but because he'd been nasty to her about it.

She finished, 'Because we obviously couldn't just go with our gut feeling when making a change like this.' Again there was that twinkle in her green eyes as she let her gaze connect for a fraction of a second with his.

He didn't deserve that at all, he thought. It was typical of her to turn an argument into a good reason to tease each other.

Trudy and Dotty nodded innocently at her words, uniting Rip and Jo once again in their own private universe. That odd, unsettling, too-nice feeling he'd had with her last night came back, just as strong.

Merril and Amanda hadn't been with the practice very long and couldn't be expected to pick up on something so intangible, but even Trudy and Dotty seemed oblivious. They were both comfortable women in their fifties, each a grandmother twice over, great friends, active in the community, discreet about patients, treasured assets to the practice, but apparently blind and deaf when it came to certain nuances in the air.

Or is it just me?

Yes, of course it was just him.

Jo didn't mean it that way. They'd known each other for five years. What could possibly have changed? He'd better get that dinner invitation out of the way as soon as possible, prove there was nothing in this, nip it in the bud before it got out of hand...

'Handing over to you now, Rip,' Jo said, after they'd decided that she would be the one to follow up on changing pathology services.

Again, their eyes met, and though he knew it was only because she was wary of getting to the meatiest part of the agenda—the issue of taking on a third partner—and because she guessed that he'd feel the same, it still gave him that...oh...that feeling again.

He didn't have a name for it.

He couldn't even describe it.

It was nothing like what he'd ever felt for Tara.

'They didn't resign on the spot, which is a good sign,' Jo said, pitching her voice low. The 'they' in question, Dotty and Trudy, were in the practice's tiny kitchen, heating leftovers for lunch in the microwave.

'Did you expect them to?' Rip leaned on the handle of his office door, making the door swing slightly. To and fro. In and out. Open and not so open.

The movement irritated Jo.

No, 'irritated' was the wrong word.

It frustrated her.

If they had more to say to each other in private, then Rip should close the door and make it clear. Otherwise, he should open it so she could nip next door to the Harriet Café and have some lunch.

Most often, she either brought a sandwich from home or drove the two and a half minutes it took her to get there and made one fresh. Leftovers from last night's evening meal heated in the microwave were not usually on her menu, because last night's evening meal was rarely substantial enough to generate any. Going to the café was a rarer option still, but she'd chosen it today as part of her strategy for climbing out of that rut she'd seen herself in so clearly last night.

Answering Rip's question, she said, 'No, but it will mean extra work for them, especially at first. It'll lighten our load, but not Dotty and Trudy's.'

'Or Merril and Amanda's, for that matter.'

'I had thought they might be a little more resistant to the idea of a third doctor.'

'I don't think they see it that way. Anything that eases our load is going to make us more relaxed, and a relaxed doctor has to be better for the practice managers than a stressed-out one.'

'Mmm. True.'

'And if we can come up with someone who comes with a personal recommendation... I'm going to make a couple of phone calls later today, get the ball rolling on that.'

'I'll give it some thought, too,' Jo promised, although so far she couldn't think of any obvious prospects.

She'd led such a quiet life here, and she'd only kept up with a couple of the people who'd gone through medicine with her. Her friendship roster in med school and residency had been slashed in half following the break-up with Jack. He'd put so much effort in getting her to fall for him, and just as much into keeping their mutual friends on his side after he'd ended it. He'd conserved his energy by expending as little as possible on the relationship itself, however.

And if that sounded cynical, well, the cynicism was hard won. It had taken her a good two or three years to be able to see him that way, and a couple more to let go of her anger. Now she'd moved on. He just wasn't important at all. It felt good, but she needed to widen her horizons. She needed more people in her life who *were* important.

Rip let the door swing open again and Jo really thought they were done. She made a move to leave and then stopped as he spoke once more. 'Anyone interesting on your list this afternoon?'

'Um, I don't think so. Pretty routine.'

'Right. Same here.' His voice shifted gear. 'If you're not busy tonight, want to do the dinner idea? My place?'

Oh.

'That would be nice,' she said, and then added, because it had sounded so insipid, 'It would be great.' She'd honestly expected him to let the whole thing slide, and she never would have thrown out any hints as a reminder. She didn't work that way.

'Seven?'

From habit, Jo's mind flipped to her TV guide. At seven on a Wednesday she usually watched—

No. Stop it, Jo.

'Seven sounds fine.'

'Good.' He smiled.

It wasn't the professional smile he gave to his patients, or the tight, strung-out smile he'd given for most of last year when people had asked him, 'How're you doing?' And it wasn't the smile Jo had seen him give Tara either—that dazzled, helpless, slow-fading grin. It was just a warm, nice smile, with trust and eye contact and the same tiny suggestion of a shared secret that she'd picked up on and shot back at him during the meeting a few minutes ago.

But somehow it did things to her insides that she wouldn't have believed possible a few days ago.

He stepped back and closed his door between them, and she went off to the Harriet Café, somehow not as hungry as she'd thought she was ten minutes earlier.

Their routine afternoon unfolded just as she'd expected, until a slightly unusual interruption, in the form of a walk-in at around three-thirty—a six-year-old girl with a splinter in her foot, accompanied by her mother, a manic toddler and a dog who had to be left outside and didn't want to be.

Jo knew about the dog because her office overlooked the flower-bed at the front of the professional building where the big black poodle was now tethered to a lamppost, obedient and quiet.

Trudy knocked discreetly at Jo's door to ask if she could squeeze the little girl in. 'The splinter's the size of a steak-knife blade, but Merril left at lunch, Dr Taylor is doing a procedure, and we had a couple of people he was with for longer than expected, so he's running behind. It's your call, Dr Middleton.'

'I'm not doing too badly,' Jo said. 'Yes, let me see her. What's her name?'

'This family isn't on our books. Apparently they've only just moved here. The child is Alice and the mother is Nina. Last name Grafton.'

'We're just up the road,' the mother explained a minute later, after she'd pushed Alice into the office in a stroller clearly meant for the little boy. 'Walking distance. I'll make an appointment for myself while I'm here, but I thought… I know it's only a splinter, but it's huge, and it's deep, and I don't drive and my husband's at work, which makes a trip to the emergency room… The hospital is, what, twenty minutes from here?'

'Twenty-five, if you keep to the speed limit,' Jo told her.

'Yes, that's the only drawback to Harriet.' Mrs Grafton frowned, as if she'd given the subject serious consideration. She looked like a nice woman, around Jo's own age, with dark hair, pale skin, intelligent eyes and a yellowing bruise on her temple. 'Otherwise I know we're going to love it here. We saw the house, so pretty, with the mountain views, and we couldn't resist, and Andy's work is less than ten minutes away. He's with the county engineer's department.'

Trudy brought in the box of blocks from the waiting room, and the little boy, Cody, began transferring them noisily to the floor.

'And anyhow an ambulance can get to the hospital in fifteen minutes in an emergency,' Jo offered, in Harriet's defence.

'Yes, well, that's what we thought, in the end.' Mrs Grafton looked as if she might say more, but then Alice gingerly lifted her foot to inspect it, and gave a hiss and a whimper as she saw again what her barefoot slip on an old shed floor had done. 'For now, this splinter. You're being so brave, Alice, sweetheart.' She kissed her daughter's hair, then mouthed over her head to Jo, 'But not for much longer, I'm warning you. Look, it's gone right beneath the skin.'

Beneath several layers of skin, it turned out. The injury really was nasty, and after a closer inspection Jo decided to do the thing properly and administer a local anaesthetic. Alice yelped and cried as the needle went in.

Her mother patted her and told her she was brave again,

but Cody had lost interest in the blocks and wanted to play doctor with the equipment in Jo's cupboards and drawers, so most of Mrs Grafton's attention went towards staying one step ahead of him.

'He's been a horror for the past six months,' she said, over her shoulder. Then she sighed and made a tut-tut sound.

Alice said suddenly, 'Mommy, do you need Jeannie to come in?'

'No, honey, it's fine.'

'Are you sure?' The six-year-old looked oddly concerned, and seemed to have forgotten her foot. The anaesthesia would be taking effect already.

To distract her as she cut into the skin, Jo asked, 'Is Jeannie your dog?'

'Yes, and she's very, very special,' Alice said. She gave another frowning glance at her mother.

'I'm sure she is,' Jo answered. 'Dogs are always special, and they love their families.'

'Jeannie's the most special. She's a poodle, and poodles are clever and Jeannie is the cleverest.'

OK, good. Jo had now made a nice-sized opening at the point of the splinter, wide enough for the back end to pass through. She didn't want to reverse direction. Much better to pull it right through the same direction it had gone in, so that with luck she wouldn't leave any barbed pieces behind.

'Tell me some of the clever things Jeannie does,' she said to Alice, to keep the child talking.

Nina was desperately trying to focus Cody's attention on the blocks, not on all those easy-to-open doors and drawers full of lovely tongue depressors and paper-sealed dressings and sample boxes which, after all, were just like blocks, only with the allure of the forbidden.

'She takes care of Mommy,' Alice said. 'Yesterday, she wouldn't let Mommy go down in the basement.'

'Was there something spooky down there?' Jo wasn't really thinking about the question.

OK, here it comes. Don't look, Alice.

Jo eased the splinter free, thinking that Trudy's description of it had been very accurate. It did look like a steak-knife blade—long, pointed, jagged and nasty.

'Is it out? I didn't feel it! When I close my eyes, my foot's not there, Mommy, and when I touch it, it's like touching a toy foot!' Alice giggled. She'd forgotten about Jo's last question, too.

'I'm going to put some cream on it now, Alice,' Jo said, as she made a final inspection to make sure she wasn't leaving any foreign matter inside the shallow wound. She found a couple of specks of dirt and deftly removed them, then asked Nina, 'Is she up to date on her tetanus?'

'Yes, but her immunisation records are in a file box somewhere, so you'll have to take my word on that!'

'Get a copy to us when you can. There's no hurry.'

'When I come in later in the week,' Mrs Grafton promised.

Jo put a light dressing on the wound, while Cody stalled on putting the blocks back in the box. In the end, his mother let him get away with a token bit of 'help' while doing most of it herself.

'He used to be such a sweetheart about things like this! Sometimes it really worries me,' she said.

'They're not terrible and two forever,' Jo answered, although she hadn't had a lot of personal experience.

The biological clock had been ticking louder of late, however. She never used to mind saying no when a parent asked her if she had kids of her own. Now she sometimes got a tightening in her chest. And she sometimes pretended that she knew more about kids than she really did. Was that pathetic, or natural?

'No, and thank goodness they're not, even though I love him to pieces,' Nina said.

She seemed like a nice woman, with a nice family, although Jo had a small, niggling question about the fading bruise on Mrs Grafton's temple. She'd noticed a couple more, including one that was fresher and bluer, along the woman's forearm. This wasn't a common red-flag location for domestic violence injuries, unless the bruise came in the shape of fingermarks, but she made a tiny, cryptic note in little Alice's file about it all the same.

With the dressing in place and the anaesthesia still keeping the area numb, Alice was happy to go off in Cody's stroller, while Cody ignored his mother's instruction to hold onto the side. She stopped at the front desk to make the appointment for herself that she'd mentioned, and Jo focused her own attention on her next patient. Running behind now, she didn't surface until nearly six.

Trudy had already gone, as had Amanda. Merril only worked mornings. Dotty was shutting off the front desk computer and taking a late call with an appointment request for tomorrow. 'He has a spot at eleven-thirty,' Jo heard her say into the phone, then she put her hand over the mouthpiece and said, 'Message for you, Dr Middleton, before you go.'

Jo waited, stretching her tired neck and spine, while a difficult negotiation over tomorrow's appointment with Dr Taylor took place. No, he didn't have anything earlier. Or anything after four-thirty. How about just before lunch?

Finally, a decision was made.

'The pathology service called,' Dotty told her, once she'd put down the phone. 'A couple of hours ago, actually. Before we had the little girl with the splinter, I think. I asked if I should get you on the line, but they said no. They said they'd call back, but they haven't.'

'What was it about, do you know?'

'Harry Brown's blood-test results from this morning.'

'I'll call them.' Jo felt a sudden prick of concern.

Harry's father, the custodial parent, had brought the five-year-old in for a ten o'clock appointment that morning. Both Harry and his dad usually saw Rip, but his schedule had been full, and Bill Brown hadn't wanted to wait. He'd been happy to see Jo instead.

'Just concerned,' he'd said. 'He seems a bit off colour, and he's got these bruises.'

It had been a day for questionable bruises, Jo thought now, with those ones she'd noticed on Alice Grafton's mother, on top of Harry's bruises earlier. Bill Brown had shown them to her, seeming genuinely worried and perplexed. 'He says he hasn't had any falls or bumps, and I don't remember any myself. But he was with his mother over the weekend. Last weekend, too, and it was after that when I first noticed them.'

He'd lowered his voice at that point and had spoken in a rush over the top of his son's head. 'You know, Dr Middleton, you can't help wondering, all the things you read about abuse. I'm not suggesting Vanessa—lord no, never—but I think she's been seeing someone new, and I'm thinking, some guy I don't even know, involved in my boy's life...'

So Jo had asked Harry some questions, but he'd insisted he hadn't hurt himself and that no one had hurt him. Wondering about his platelet count as a possible cause, she'd ordered a full blood count and a clotting test, and had asked for a quick turnaround on the result, which would mean she'd have it by the end of the day.

Why would the pathology lab have called once and not followed up?

She went back into her office and picked up the phone.

When she put it down again twenty minutes later, she was steaming.

And she was scared.

Dotty had gone but Rip's office door was still slightly ajar and she heard his swivel chair creak. She went in to him at once and saw him quickly fold a piece of printed paper. His face looked tired and tight, and it was probably lucky that she had something urgent on her mind or she would have had a hard time fighting a need to go up to him and soften away the tightness with her fingers, the way a potter worked fresh clay.

'Rip?' she said. 'Do you have any more contact details on Harry Brown, other than his home address with his dad and his mother's place in Rutland, and their various phone numbers? I mean, there's nothing in either of their files, but something anecdotal? Bill is usually your patient, so I thought you might.'

'What's the problem?'

'I got those results back on Harry's blood tests from this morning. He has a platelet count of two.'

'My lord! Two?' A normal, healthy count should be between one and two hundred, anything below about forty was a serious concern, and a count this low was life-threatening. 'The lab just called with it now?'

'No, I called them.'

'You shouldn't have had to—'

'No. Exactly. Someone—a doctor whose name I didn't recognise—had called at around three when I was in the middle of a procedure. He declined Dotty's offer to put me on the line and said he would call back, which she correctly interpreted as an indication that it wasn't urgent.'

Rip made a disgusted sound.

'Yeah, I know,' Jo said. 'Because it is urgent, incredibly urgent, and he didn't call back. As soon as Dotty told me—and thank goodness she did—I called him and got a result that we should have heard about as a number-one priority the moment they had it.'

'And the service can't blame that on their chronic shortage of cyto technicians.'

'No, they can't. It's a huge stuff-up, and I'm really worried now. I've tried Harry's dad's house, his work, his ex-wife, her cellphone, his cellphone, and I'm getting nothing. No pickup. No machine. Cells switched off. I've left a message at his work number and on both their cells—'

'While Harry has a platelet count of two.' Rip stood up, his tension transformed into active energy. They both understood the significance of the figure. 'That child could practically bleed to death from a bruised shin.'

'Or have an intracranial hemorrhage in his sleep tonight. He presented with unexplained bruising, but it wasn't dramatic. Bill was concerned about non-accidental injury, and I'm wondering if that led me astray? Did I focus on the wrong thing? Should I have sent it to the stat lab at Duchesne County Memorial? His ex-wife has a new partner. I ordered a full blood count, but it was more to rule out a platelet problem, not to confirm it. Whether this is more my fault than the lab's or not, I'm not prepared to let this go till the morning, Rip.'

'Of course not.'

'We have to get hold of the family and get Harry admitted. I'd like to give the news in person, but at this stage I'd take a carrier pigeon rather than waste any more time. You've seen the dad a few times, haven't you?'

'Yes, five or six, since I joined the practice.'

'Hasn't he said anything useful? Are there grandparents

in the area? I looked up Brown in the phone directory but there are a gazillion of them, and we don't have the mother's maiden name in the file.'

'I think it was Brown.' Ripley wiped a hand around the back of his neck as he spoke, massaging the tightness away.

Jo's turn to frown. 'What?'

'I think that's how they met. On some tour. The tour guide thought they were a couple because they were both called— It's not important. Let me think. Bill Brown has a fishing cabin on the Franklin River, near Sherrington. Would he have gone there midweek?'

'He was worried about Harry's health. Talked about him being off colour. Maybe he thought some wild mountain air...'

'From what he said about it, I doubt there's a phone.'

As if the word 'phone' was a cue, the instrument rang out at the front desk. Jo dashed to it to pick it up before the machine clicked on, because Dotty would already have set it for overnight. 'Hello, Harriet Family Medicine Center, Dr Middleton speaking.'

'Hi, Dr Middleton, this is Vanessa Brown...'

Harry's mother had gotten the message Jo had left on her cellphone. That was the good news. The bad news was that she had no idea where Harry and Bill were, except that they wouldn't be at either set of grandparents because her parents were away and Bill's were both in a nursing home.

Ms Brown had stressed at the beginning of the call that she was not the custodial parent, which Jo already knew. She sounded busy, tired and impatient, until Jo explained, as gently as she could without understating the case, that Harry's platelet count was catastrophically low. It didn't matter why, at this stage, although that would be determined as quickly as possible. The critical issue was the danger of a serious bleed. Harry needed hospital treatment as soon as he could get it.

'Oh. Oh. Oh,' Vanessa said, and Jo could almost hear the grind of shifting gears as her important state government job suddenly ceased to matter and her son became the only thing in her life that did. 'Where will he go? Duchesne County Memorial?'

'Yes, as soon as we track him down. Dr Taylor wondered if he and his father could be at a fishing cabin near—'

'Sherrington. There's no phone. It's crazy. Bill switches off his cell. If it's even in range out there. I'll kill him. Yes, he could well be there. Or anywhere. They go off on these wild...' She made a frustrated sound. 'He teaches Harry way more than he learns at school, he's an incredible parent, but it's still crazy, and when something like this...' She cut herself off again. 'Let me give you directions. Try the cabin first.'

Rip raised his eyebrows at Jo the moment she got off the phone.

'We're trying the cabin first,' she said. 'His mother is driving up from Rutland and she'll meet Harry at the hospital. Assuming we've found him and sent him there. I left my cell number on the messages I left for Bill, so he may call back as we're driving.'

'I've locked up. Let's go.' He put his hand to his head as he turned.

'Are you OK, Rip?'

'Will you stop asking me that?' He stopped abruptly in the doorway and she almost ran into him. For a moment her hand hovered near his shoulder blade but she managed to pull back without making contact. The breath felt too full in her lungs suddenly, and when she let it out, it wasn't quite steady.

'Only if you answer,' she said.

'I have a headache, that's all.' He stepped aside to let her pass through, then closed and locked the door behind him, which gave her a moment to study him.

She'd begun to take notice of things about him that she'd never been interested in before. When had that started? They were, oh, trivial things, too—physical details like the sturdy length and bulk of his forearms, the angle of his neck when he bent his head, and the way his dark hair sat so neat against his head behind his ears.

And for some time she'd known him well enough to be able to guess, quite often, what he was thinking. She could do it now. 'That sheet of paper you were looking at when I came in, that was…?'

'Yes, the patient information leaflet that comes with the nicotine patch. Classic case of doctors making the worst patients. I'm dreaming up a nicotine overdose on the basis of one slight symptom.'

'I'll keep an eye on you,' Jo told him. 'Meanwhile, take something for the headache.'

'Now you're patronising me. I already did.'

'Are we arguing again, Rip?' She didn't really mind if they were. She quite liked arguing with him.

He sighed. 'Problem is, the patch only takes care of the physical symptoms, not the psychological ones. I'm…' He searched for the right word. 'Disappointed that I'm not finding this easier.'

He reached his car, parked next to Jo's on the little apron of tar to the side of the professional building that was reserved for doctors. Jo patted his shoulder and he glanced down at the place where her hand rested, then looked up at her face. Another one of those moments.

Moments of contact.

New.

She took her hand away and said, 'You're doing really well. Don't be so hard on yourself.'

If he appreciated her concern, he didn't say so. 'There's no point in taking two cars. We'll use mine.'

Neither of them was on call tonight. The Harriet Family Medicine Center rotated on call periods with the newer two-doctor practice in the neighbouring town of Netherby, and this was one of their nights.

'So we're both going?' Jo said, and wished at once that she hadn't.

His car yelped as he pressed the button on his key fob to unlock the door. He looked at the key fob, not at Jo, as if the automatic car door opening technology was way more fascinating.

'You said "we" after you'd talked to Vanessa Brown.' He spoke slowly. 'I assumed you wanted help in finding the place. And since our dinner's obviously postponed... But if you're happy to go alone, that's fine, too.'

She didn't want the decision left up to her. She wanted his company, but she didn't want to have to say it in case she sounded as if she wanted his company too much. And she was a bit unsettled about *why* she wanted his company so much, and that was just ridiculous all round!

She stayed helplessly silent for a second too long, and Rip said, 'Look, this is stupid.'

Which it was.

Stupid and ridiculous.

They agreed on that, at least.

'I'm coming, Jo, OK? I'm driving. There's a map in the glove compartment. Using that and the directions from Harry's mother, it's your job to get us there. Later, if we get a good outcome on this, we'll drive into Burlington for a late meal. Take-out pizza or drive-through burgers, if it comes down to that. Is that a plan?'

'It's a good plan.'

Settling back into the front passenger seat, she didn't dare say anything until she'd talked herself out of this fluttery feeling in her stomach, and that task took far longer than it should have done.

CHAPTER FOUR

'It's pitch dark,' Jo said.

'It's the cloud cover, and there's no moon unfortunately.'

'Can you go a little slower, Rip? There's supposed to be a turn-off coming up. Vanessa said there used to be a couple of red reflectors on the sign but she hasn't been here for several years so she couldn't promise that the sign was the same.'

'I'm glad we're in late March, not January. I'm starting to see snow beside the road from those falls last week. If we get any higher up, and onto a track that hasn't been cleared—'

'Here!' She'd glimpsed some circles of red, flaring out like eyes when the beam from Rip's headlights hit them. 'Yes, it says Brown. This is the place. She says the track winds in for a couple of hundred yards.'

'Can you see any lights?' Rip asked.

'Not yet. Keep driving. I don't know what our next move will be if no one's there. I feel as if we're bomb-disposal experts, and we know the timer is ticking down but we can't find the bomb.'

'I know.' His teeth were clenched. 'Do you want to know how much I'm punishing myself for not taking more notice of the pathology service's quality? To be honest, I thought it was just me—impatient, on a short fuse, spoiling for a fight with anyone I could find.'

'Don't, Rip. It was gradual, and there's been nothing flagrantly irresponsible until now. Ironic that it should happen today, when we'd already decided to make a change.

I was to blame, too, for not putting a more urgent priority on the tests. And anyhow, as you said, you've had...things on your mind this past year or so.'

'That's no excuse. If I was dropping the ball, I should have taken time off. You should have called me on it.'

'*Called* you? We felt for you, Rip!'

'You shouldn't have. I should have kept my private problems separate from my work.'

'You did.'

'I didn't. Not always. Sometimes it was an act.'

'Give Hollywood a call, then, because you were good.'

He made a frustrated sound, and she felt helpless again. Helpless about how she felt now, and about how she should have acted in the past. There was an intimacy to them being enclosed in his car together like this in the gathering darkness, both of them impatient and aware of the urgency of their mission. She felt as if their relationship had suddenly arrived at a critical balance point which made everything they said to each other significant in a way it had never been before.

'Snow,' he said a moment later. 'There *is* snow. Damn! This car does snow like a figure skater.' It was the one Tara had usually driven, Jo knew—the one he should probably sell if he was truly committed to moving on after the divorce. 'We should have stopped at my place on the way,' he went on, 'and swapped for the SUV.'

He tightened his grip on the wheel as the vehicle careened across an old drift of snow that had melted in the sun and refrozen as ice. After slithering dangerously close to the trunk of a pine, they cleared the stand of trees and the track became mud again, rutted but far less slippery.

'And there's a light,' Jo said.

She glimpsed it through the trees then lost it again.

Her stomach rumbled. It was after seven.

She and Rip should have been at his house, sipping a drink, while he... The image in her mind shut down as she realised she had no idea if he cooked, or got take-out every night, or ate peanut butter on toast.

Well, he wouldn't cater peanut butter on toast for a guest, even if it was just his professional partner, but the range of possible options stayed wide and she couldn't picture how their scheduled evening would have played out.

Not like current reality, for certain.

The light flickered back into view, the trees seemed to part like spreading fingers and they emerged into a snow-drifted clearing.

'Looks like a decent place,' Rip said. 'And I can smell food cooking. Something with garlic.'

He brought his car to a halt right in front of the cabin, and they both jumped out. Bill must have heard the engine noise, because the front door had already opened to spill yellow light across the wooden porch as they came up the short flight of steps, moving almost at a run. Temporarily blinded by the darkness of night and a cloudy sky, Harry's father peered out, trying to identify his unexpected visitors. He was a solidly built man, at home out of doors, intelligent but stubborn, Jo had gathered.

The sight of him filled her with a mix of relief because he was actually here—he easily might not have been—and dread because of what they had to tell him. And the danger didn't end with the telling. Harry needed hospital treatment, and that was three quarters of an hour away from this place.

'It's Dr Taylor, Bill, and Dr Middleton,' Rip said. Recognition dawned on Bill's face as the two doctors reached the spilling light. Bill and Rip both stuck out their hands for a brief handshake. 'I'm sorry to spring a visit on you like this, but we couldn't seem to get hold of you any other way. You've got Harry here?'

'Eating his dinner. Spaghetti and...' Bill's face paled suddenly. 'His mother's all right, is she? No, they'd send the police for something like that. An accident, or— It's his tests. Is it his tests? Hell, I should have called tonight!'

'A problem did show up, yes,' Rip began carefully.

Too carefully. He'd given Bill's thoughts enough time to go racing ahead.

'For you to have chased us up all the way out here, after dark, both of you...' He sagged against the doorframe as if his legs were about to give way from under him. It was painfully clear how much his son meant to him. Rip stepped closer, alert to the possibility of him falling.

'He's all right, Bill,' Jo said. 'There's a very good chance he'll be all right if we can get him to the hospital right away, and get treatment started. He has an extremely low platelet count—'

'Why? Are you saying it's cancer?'

'No, we don't know yet. There are a few possibilities, most of which have good outcomes in most cases.'

'OK, so...' Bill's breathing was shallow. He wanted answers faster and clearer than Jo or Rip could give them.

'At this stage,' Rip said, 'we're more concerned about the possibility of dangerous bleeding.'

'If he hurts himself? You mean more of those bruises?'

'It could happen internally, without any injury. We want to check him and get him to the hospital tonight, get him started on treatment and tests, but it's been hard to track you down.'

'What kind of treatment and tests?'

'IV platelets to get his count back up, an aspiration of his bone marrow, immunology blood tests, to get a diagnosis. Look, let's save this level of detail for later.'

'You've talked to Vanessa?' Bill's breath steamed in the

cold air, and he hadn't yet gathered his control enough to invite them inside.

'Yes, she gave us directions,' Jo said.

'Is she coming up? Did she say? He only sees her every couple of weeks, but he's close to her.'

'She's meeting you at the hospital. Now that we know you're here, we'll call the ambulance and—'

'I should never have brought him here, not till I'd heard about the tests. I thought the break might do him good, or I might get something more from him about the bruises if we were on our own. Hell, you know, at some level I almost *wanted* to think Vanessa's new boyfriend might be that kind of guy.' He shook his head, disgusted with himself.

'Don't think about that now,' Jo said.

'We're not in cellphone range. I was going to drive down and phone your office first thing in the morning. You have to get almost to Sherrington.'

Rip and Jo exchanged glances.

'I'll go,' he told her. 'Bill, Dr Middleton will stay here with you and talk to Harry about what's happening, answer your questions. I won't waste time on this, I'll head back down toward Sherrington now. With the ambulance station in Pagineau, it won't take them long to get here, but then Harry will have to go down to Duchesne County Memorial.'

'Come in, Dr Middleton,' Bill invited her vaguely, at last. Rip had already thumped down the steps to his car. 'They'd better drive fast, those paramedics... Harry?' He went over and hugged his son gently, hardly touching him, concerned about how fragile he was. Then he bent his tall body so that he and Harry were at eye level. 'Got some news, buddy, about those tests you had.'

* * *

The wait for the ambulance was tense, despite the inviting warmth and colourful clutter of the open-plan cabin. Bill managed to pack some things for himself as well as Harry, and Jo encouraged the little boy to finish his meal. While he did so, she gave him a quick visual check, and her stomach dropped a little further when she found that one of his knee joints was swollen.

'Does it hurt, Harry? Your knee's all swollen—is it hurting?' She palpated it gently—he was still chewing a last mouthful of spaghetti—and he nodded. 'Why didn't you tell your dad, honey?'

He shrugged, gave a crooked grin and said, 'Don't know.'

'You didn't think about it? Are you a little tough guy?'

'Dad says I'm tough.'

Jo could imagine Bill taking pride in the fact also. While keeping a close eye on the child, particularly in regard to the mother's new boyfriend, he wouldn't have encouraged complaints.

'Let's put some ice on it,' she told Harry.

Bill arrived back in the room with their packed bags, and she sent him to the freezer for a packet of peas. The paramedics would have a better ice pack, and the sooner they got here, the better.

Rip arrived first, with the news that the emergency vehicle was on its way. 'Lights and sirens. They'd been having a quiet night.'

'That's good,' Jo said.

'Should only be about ten minutes. Maybe less. I'm going to head back out to the turn-off to direct them.'

'Car still skating on that snow patch?'

'Not now that I know when it's coming. I'll follow the ambulance back in.'

'Tell them about the snow, too.'

There was little that the paramedics could do for Harry on the spot. Getting him to the hospital as fast as possible was their top priority. Bill would be able to accompany his son in the back of the vehicle.

'Are you coming to the hospital, Dr Taylor?' he asked. 'Dr Middleton?'

Rip flicked a quick glance at Jo, and she gave a tiny nod. There was no real need or obligation for them to go, but she shared Rip's feeling that they should see this through, and that they wanted to, after the dangerously slack communication from the pathology service and Jo's own questions about how she'd underestimated the significance of the bruising.

'Yes, we'll make sure you're settled in safely,' Rip said.

'I hope Vanessa's there. If some after-hours crisis has come up in her precious department...'

'She was planning to drive up right away, I think,' Jo answered as neutrally as she could.

A family doctor couldn't afford to take sides in this kind of issue between divorced parents. Three feet away from Rip, she could almost feel him thinking what he'd voiced aloud numerous times over the past year and a half—thank heaven that at least he and Tara hadn't had kids. Jo couldn't help wondering if Tara ever saw their break-up in those terms.

He and Jo followed the ambulance as far as the end of the track, then it powered ahead of them along the much smoother and faster roads that led towards the interstate highway and then west in the direction of Burlington.

Still dressed in a neat business suit, with her blonde hair in a low knot on her neck, Vanessa was waiting at the hospital. Bill had gone straight in to the paediatric section of the emergency department with Harry and the paramedics, and had only just come out to the waiting area, to find her pacing there, with little idea of what was going on. Somehow the busy desk staff hadn't yet let her know that her son and ex-husband had arrived.

'You're here,' Bill said. 'Thanks, Nessa, for doing this. I mean that.'

She wasn't impressed, and her voice dropped to an irate mutter. 'I'm not here as a favour, Bill, I'm his mother. I've been pacing in front of this triage desk for nearly an hour, not knowing when he'd get here, or how he was, or what was happening. I've tried your cellphone at least six times, but you never switched it on.'

'Lord, sorry! I was too panicked to think straight.'

'They gave me one or two updates on the ambulance, but there wasn't much detail. He had some bleeding in a joint, they said. Is that serious? I'm a mess. I'm...'

Shaking, Jo saw.

Bill touched Vanessa's arm. 'Yeah, yeah, I know. I'm sorry. Of course you are. Let's go and sit with him. Can we do that, Dr Middleton?'

'Yes, let me get someone to show you through.'

'They've got the doctor coming down,' Bill told Vanessa. 'Couple of doctors, I think.'

At the ER nurses' station, Rip and Jo spoke to the paediatric resident briefly, outlining Harry's history, the bruising, the tests, the platelet count, the chase up to the cabin in the woods, and the way-too-casual reporting of the pathology service doctor that afternoon. This hospital did not use the same service.

'We won't be either, as soon as we can make a switch,' Rip said. 'This shouldn't have happened. We could have gotten him here four hours ago if the lab had had their eye on the ball.'

Four hours that could still mean the difference between life and death, Jo knew.

'Any signs that he has had a further bleed anywhere?' the resident asked.

'No, just the left knee joint,' Jo said.

'Still, we're taking no chances. We're going to get platelets into him right away.'

'But he's not safely out of the woods yet.' Saying it out loud made her heart kick, and she knew she had to let her fear go.

'Hey, at least he's safely out of the woods—I mean the actual woods woods,' the resident joked lamely.

'The isolated location was a complication we didn't need,' Rip agreed.

'So's my humour, people tell me. Let me see what we can do with this kid...'

He went back into the cubicle where Harry and his parents were now talking to a nurse. She had set up a transfusion of platelets, and the pathologist had just arrived, stopping to say a brief word to Rip and Jo. She would perform the bone-marrow aspiration right away, going in through the sternum where only minimal bleeding would result from the procedure.

'Are you OK?' Rip asked Jo, a few minutes later, on their way out to the car. 'I'd like to call the hospital later on for an update, but for now...'

'I'm still a bit jittery, but you're right, there's nothing more we can do at our end.' She spread her hands and sighed. 'I wish there was.'

'And it doesn't stop us from thinking about it,' Rip said.

'Is your likely scenario the same as mine? I mean, your diagnosis. I don't want to think about bleeding in the brain. I just can't!'

'Idiopathic thrombocytopenic purpura. You're right, don't think about more serious bleeds.'

'The name of the ailment is a nice mouthful!' She gave a shaky laugh. 'His parents are going to love it.'

'That's if the immunology tests are negative and the bone-marrow aspiration shows a high number of platelet precursors. It would be the most common cause of a count that low, coming on so fast, and it's treatable.'

The cause of the condition wasn't yet fully understood. It was known to be an auto-immune disease in which antibodies attacked the body's own platelets. In older people it could be triggered by certain medications such as quinine, but in children like Harry the prevailing theory was that it was a post-viral complication resulting from an overproduction of antibodies.

Rip knew that Harry would need medication to suppress his immune response, and that he'd be kept in the hospital until his platelet count rose to a safer level. Probably over forty, which should take two or three days. He'd come back to their practice for daily blood tests to follow up on his platelet count, and if the level continued to rise he would be fine. If Harry didn't respond adequately, the next step would be the removal of his spleen.

Rip hoped they wouldn't need to go that far, and for now he let the whole issue go. You just couldn't obsess about a patient who was out of your own hands and in the care of hospital staff, even when that patient was a child. Especially then, in fact.

Jo was still upset, though, he could see.

'Look, he's got platelets going in,' he said, and brushed a strand of her hair away from the corner of her mouth. She looked as if she might start sucking on it at any minute, like a twelve-year-old before a school examination. 'With every minute that passes, the danger is less. Let's find a way to make those minutes pass as quickly as possible.'

'Miracle worker! You can speed up time?'

'With both hands tied behind my back. No, but it's almost eight-thirty and we haven't eaten. Are we still up for dinner in Burlington? There's a nice place on the river, where we can relax and watch the water.'

'Oh, if it's the one I'm thinking of, yes. It's very nice.'

'And it lets my cooking off the hook.'

'Why? Aren't you any good?' she teased.

'I'm great with the basics, but it's fatal when I try to impress.'

'But that's OK, because you wouldn't have tried to impress me,' she decided on his behalf.

Wouldn't I? Rip wondered as he started his car yet again.

You mean I wouldn't have secretly dashed out during what was supposed to be lunch today to stock up on asparagus and filet mignon and cream and cooking chocolate? I wouldn't already have put wine in the fridge? And raced around like a crazy man, plumping up all those throw pillows that Tara left behind?

His heart sank.

Do Jo and I know each other too well in all the wrong ways?

What is it that I'm hoping for here?

Jo seemed a heck of a lot more relaxed about it than he felt. Maybe she was still keeping her tension in reserve over the question of Harry Brown's health. Or maybe she'd taken genuine comfort from his reassurance to her earlier. He liked that idea a little too much—that he had a positive influence on her spirits.

When they were seated at the restaurant, taking a just-vacated table for two by the huge windows over the water, she studied her menu hungrily. 'Lunch was too small and too long ago, I'm telling you!'

'Order up big, then. It's on me.'

'Oh? Why?' Now she suddenly looked alarmed, and he

remembered how scrupulous they'd always been in the past, on the rare occasions when they'd eaten out together or in a group, to split the tab.

This didn't quite explain the alarm.

Hell, does she think I'm going to expect payment in kind later on?

What an attractive idea, said the part of him that did its thinking below his belt.

'Because this was supposed to happen at my place,' he said. 'When obviously it would have been on me.'

Had he managed to hide how totally knocked for a loop he'd just been by the power of that very male, very physical fantasy?

'I'm not sure that I quite buy your reasoning, but thanks anyway. In that case, I won't order the whole Maine lobster, the truffles or the French champagne.'

'Jo, for heaven's sake, order what you like!'

'Kidding, Ripley.' She took a slightly unsteady breath. 'Although I'm not surprised that you didn't pick up on it. I think we're both...kind of missing things with each other tonight.'

She made a little gesture with her index fingers, pushing their tips towards each other but letting them pass without touching.

Missed connections.

Different wavelengths.

Speaking a different language.

She looked over the fingers and smiled at him, and he almost...*almost*...reached across the table to take her hand.

Take it slow, he coached himself. Work out if you really want this or if you don't, because it'll be disastrous if you find out that you don't want it *after* you've made a move.

A move?

On Jo?

Lord, this wasn't a singles bar, and he wasn't in his twenties any more, the way he'd been when he and Tara had met. Wasn't this sort of thing supposed to get easier with age, maturity and bitter experience?

Apparently it didn't. Another illusion shattered.

'On second thoughts, though, French champagne would be nice,' Jo said slyly across the table.

'This time, I'm not going to let you get away with a claim that you're kidding, Dr Middleton.'

'Hey, no—'

'Yes.' He opened the wine list and deliberately chose something with a famous name and an expensive price tag, calling her bluff.

It was very good champagne, even though with a half-hour night-time drive ahead of him, Rip only allowed himself half a glass.

The food was very good, too.

And the conversation was great, because the food and the champagne helped them both to relax again. They didn't leave until after ten-thirty, and didn't get back to Harriet until eleven-fifteen. Beside Ripley in the passenger seat, Jo suppressed yawns all the way.

The suppressing was bad enough.

The apologising for the yawns was worse.

'I'm really sorry, Rip. That champagne made me nicely buzzy while we were eating, but now it's making me sleepy.'

'Shall I drop you home, then?' he suggested stoically, wondering if he'd ever remember how to feel sleepy again. Was she actively bored in his company, or merely relaxed? 'You can walk down in the morning, or I can come by and run you in.'

In fact, if you say the word, I've just woken up even more and I need not go back to my place at all...

Why this? Why now? Tara's departure had flattened his level of desire for more than a year. Why should it suddenly flare like this—like an illness—and attach itself to someone like Jo?

'I'll walk if the sun's out,' she said. 'I'll need the exercise, after that meal. Thanks, it was wonderful.'

'Yes, I thought so,' he said. 'We'll have to do it again. I mean, I have a bunch of asparagus and a packet of filet mignon in my fridge, thanks to the change in plan, and the asparagus won't keep. Neither will the cream. So…'

'I thought you weren't going to impress me.'

'That was your idea. That I wasn't, I mean.'

'So you *were* going to impress me?'

He bit the bullet and admitted, 'I did have an impressing-you type impulse over lunch, after our meeting, yes, and I acted on it in the supermarket. Could be disastrous…'

'Oh! Oh…' She laughed, and the sound was huskier than usual. 'How nice. How out of character.'

'Really?'

'Um, yes, out of character between you and me, don't you think? To go to that sort of trouble? Not generally, Rip. I'm not implying you're inconsiderate or— I don't know…'

Turning into her street, he felt her hand on his shoulder. She'd touched him there earlier, standing beside his car before they'd gone in search of Harry and his father. Then it had been a comforting, sympathetic gesture, but it felt a little different this time. Tentative. Questioning.

Do you like this, Rip?

Do you want me to do this?

Do you want me to do more than this?

He froze.

Yes, I very much want you to do this. And, yes, I want so much more than this from you tonight that I think I could explode if I got within twenty yards of a naked flame. But we're in partnership together, and for five years that partnership has run smoother and with less effort than my marriage ever did, and if we blow all that now by changing the ground rules between us...changing everything...then what's left?

'Thanks,' he said, and took his hand off the wheel just long enough to lay it on top of hers for half a second and no more.

Her street wasn't a long one. It climbed towards a sloping ridge, and her house was situated just at the start of the climb. He indicated a left turn into her driveway, even though there was no other traffic at this time of night, and brought the car to a halt, still thinking about kissing her, still not knowing if he was going to do it, wanting to do it with every cell in his body, fighting with himself over it, wondering how it would feel and if it could possibly answer any of his questions truthfully.

Kisses could tell such massive lies.

If he switches off the engine, Jo thought, is that a statement of intent?

She held her breath without even realising it, until the engine had gone on humming in her driveway for a few more seconds. Rip's hand hadn't moved towards the keys dangling from the ignition. He hadn't leaned closer. He hadn't looked towards her dark porch with a hopeful expression on his face.

Carefully, she let the breath out, took another one and said, 'Thanks for a really nice evening, Ripley. For a man who's just given up smoking, you did incredibly well. I'm proud of you.'

Jo Middleton, you coward!

Yep, she'd made a strategic retreat to her role as concerned professional partner, after that small neck-sticking-out moment of bravery in touching his shoulder, down at the bottom of the hill.

But maybe the strategic retreat was wise rather than cowardly. She'd given him a pretty clear signal, and he was letting it go. Any red-blooded American male with even half of Rip's reasons to feel confident about himself wouldn't need any more encouragement than she'd just given him. She didn't need to hammer the point home and earn herself a more clearly spelled-out rejection.

'Proud of me?' he echoed.

'Yes. You know, like a cheer-leader. Go, team!' She made a fist in the air. 'Kick that habit! Beat that nicotine! I should do a dance routine for you in the driveway.'

Shut up now, Jo.

He'd grinned, thank goodness. Even in the darkness, his eyes glinted. She found their light magnetic, and was so close to snapping her cards—a thick double pack of them—right down in front of her, table or not.

Kiss me, Rip, go on. If I lean into you, won't you do it? Please? If I touch you again? Maybe lay my hand against the side of your face because I love the shape of your jaw—when did that start?—and I want to know how it feels.

Won't you switch off the engine and come inside with me, kiss me in the dark and take all the decision-making and all the courage into your own hands and not leave me with any choices to make? Can't you see that I'm not breathing?

'I've never seen you dance,' he said.

'Because I can't, so I don't.' And, please, don't make the word 'dance' feel so much like the word 'kiss'.

'I bet you could.'

'I'm not doing a cheer-leader routine for you, Ripley.'

'Hey, it was your idea...'

It was my escape hatch. This time I won't try to be clever, I'll just go with the car door instead.

She opened it, letting in a flood of ardour-dampening cold air that only made her want to snuggle closer to him.

'Changed my mind,' she told him lightly.

'The cloud cover is thickening, and there was snow in the forecast. I'll pick you up in the morning,' he answered.

'If the forecast is right, that would be great.'

Come half an hour early and I'll give you coffee and pancakes.

But she'd given up now, so she didn't say it. Whatever she thought she'd seen in him tonight, echoing the bewildering and sudden change in her own feelings, she either hadn't seen it at all or it had been a momentary madness in him, and it had gone.

During the following morning, they received a report by phone from Duchesne County Memorial on Harry Brown. As they'd tentatively predicted, the results on the bone-marrow aspiration and immunology tests pointed to idiopathic thrombocytopenic purpura, and he'd begun treatment with immunosuppressant drugs. He'd had some further bleeding in his joints overnight, but no evidence of a haemorrhage in the brain. With the continued infusion of platelets, he should be out of danger now.

Jo and Rip admitted to each other that their sighs of relief went pretty deep.

Ripley spent his lunch-hour following up possibilities for the practice's third partner. He made a string of calls, glad of the chance to keep his thoughts away from Jo. They'd been straying to her even when he hadn't given them permission to do so.

It was crazy.

Spring had a lot to answer for—all those changes in the

air that Thornton Liddle had talked about a couple of days ago.

Jo had haunted Ripley's sleep the previous night, and though he would swear he'd only begun to think of her in this new and dangerous light less than forty-eight hours ago, it didn't feel that way. It felt like something he'd known about her inside himself forever.

Give yourself time, he told himself. Don't act like a teenager. Don't jump in with both feet the way you did with Tara. She was that kind of a person. Jo isn't. She needs you to play it as straight and steady as you can. She doesn't need you to make some wrong-headed mistake.

So he sensibly made phone calls to colleagues of colleagues and struck lucky on about call number nine, when he spoke to Dr Shelley Breck, whose number had been given to him by a mutual friend.

'She keeps in touch with quite a few people, she may know of someone, and I trust her judgement,' the friend had said. 'I'll let her tell you what she's doing these days.'

Ripley had been at medical school with Shelley and he'd always liked her, though they'd been classmates more than friends. She'd married young and gotten divorced in about their second or third year, which he'd assumed to be the result of the enormous pressure of their student workload.

He remembered her saying unequivocally at the time, 'When it's wrong, it's just wrong!' He didn't necessarily agree with that, but her divorce made him feel as if they had something in common now, like war veterans who'd fought in the same battle, even when he learned that Shelley was well over the long-ago life hiccup now, and married to someone else.

Rip heard that Shelley and her husband Lloyd, a writer, had just adopted Lloyd's infant great-niece, after a protracted and unsuccessful quest to solve Shelley's infertility problems, which had been unresponsive to six cycles of IVF.

'So if you're calling because you want Alan Grover's phone number or something, then you've just gotten a way bigger information dump than you were looking for, haven't you?' Shelley finished, on a warm, open laugh.

'Why would I want Alan Grover's phone number?' Rip barely remembered the man, another student in their year.

'First name that popped into my head. Why are you calling, Ripley?'

He explained briefly, and Shelley surprised him by saying that she could well be interested in the partnership position herself. It was proving stressful to her husband's niece to be living so close to the baby she'd given up.

'Michaela wants some involvement, but she needs distance also,' Shelley explained. 'She's only sixteen, and none of this has been easy for her. Lloyd and I have been talking about a move.'

'You'd be interested in Vermont?'

'A change of pace from New Jersey, I know, but it's about the right distance for Michaela. She'll be able to come up for a weekend occasionally to see the baby, but she won't be involved on a day-to-day basis, distracting her from school.'

'It must have been a pretty big step for you to adopt close to home like that,' Rip said.

'A big step, but a win-win situation, we're hoping. Mickie wouldn't have given the baby up completely, but she would have struggled as a single parent. Her own mother, Lloyd's sister, is supportive but realistic. She has a lot on her plate and was pretty ambivalent about Mickie keeping Hayley. Meanwhile, Lloyd is having great fantasies about a rustic artist's studio and a slow-paced lifestyle, which we both expect to discover are totally naïve once we actually settle on somewhere.'

'Vermont is pretty good at rustic and slow.'

'Having a job to slot right into is a big plus, too. I've only been filling in at my current practice for the past couple of months, and the regular doctor's due back any day. We can sublet our apartment and make the move right away. Should I fax you my résumé and come up for a proper meeting? No, on second thoughts, one step at a time. Show your partner my résumé and see what she thinks.'

Jo thought Shelley sounded perfect when Rip came into her office during a temporary lull late in the day to report the results of his telephone quest. 'Especially if she can laugh about her own naïve view of rural life. I appreciate people who know how to laugh at themselves.'

She was trying to laugh at herself today—at how hot and jittery she became as soon as she saw Ripley, at how driving the short distance between her place and the practice in his car suddenly seemed like an interlude to treasure in her memory for weeks.

She'd replayed their conversation several times in her head during the morning, over lunch and through most of the afternoon, replayed his smile, replayed something she'd said that had made him nod and say, 'I totally agree with you.'

'Wait till you've seen her résumé,' Rip said. 'She's faxing it up by tomorrow. If you still approve, I'll call her and arrange a time for her to come up.'

'As soon as she wants to, don't you think? Everyone seems ripe for a change in their lives this week.'

'Must be spring in the air. One of my patients said something—'

They both heard urgent sounds out in the waiting room at that moment—a dog barking, a child screaming, a half-hysterical mother—distracting Ripley so that he didn't finish. He opened Jo's office door and said quickly, 'What's up, Trudy?'

'My son,' gasped a woman's voice.

Following Rip from the room, Jo recognised the mother of yesterday's walk-in splinter removal, but she didn't have time to say hello or bring the woman's name to mind. Against the background of the toddler's shrieking cries and the six-year-old...of course, her name was Alice, Jo remembered...who was in tears now, too, as she begged Dotty to let the dog, Jeannie, stay inside, Alice's mother suddenly dropped to the floor in a full epileptic seizure.

CHAPTER FIVE

'Jo, you take the child and I'll take the mother,' Rip said. 'I think she got a good bump on the head just now when she fell. Dotty...or Jo...talk to Alice, see if we can make sense of this.'

'We should all talk to Alice,' Jo said, at the same time dropping to the stroller and trying to unwrap a drenched cotton comforter from the two-year-old boy.

It was cloudy and cold today, with snow flurries in the air. The sky already looked dark even though it was not yet five in the afternoon. Since this was the last week in March, spring had arrived according to the calendar, but you wouldn't know it outside.

Why did Mrs Grafton have Cody soaking wet like this? He was shaking and screaming. With cold, or something else?

Jo struggled with the stroller's safety straps. They were wet and slippery from the soaking fabric, and she couldn't get them undone. With Rip working over Nina, Cody crying, and Alice and Jeannie both hovering anxiously, the atmosphere didn't make it easy for Jo to focus on an unfamiliar task.

Alice was trying to explain something, but she was distressed and distracted and needed a clear question.

'Alice, honey, can you tell us why your mommy brought your brother in?' Jo asked. 'Why is he wet like this?'

Rip had knelt beside Nina Grafton, yelling to Trudy to grab pillows from the treatment room and to Dotty to call an ambulance. Mrs Grafton's body gave a series of rigid shudders and jerks, which he didn't try to restrain. There were three patients waiting, and they all looked appalled, uncertain whether to offer to help. After a few seconds it must have seemed obvious to them that the best thing to do was simply stay where they were, out of the way.

Listening to Alice, Jo narrowed her focus on the two children.

'Because Jeannie wouldn't go sit,' Alice said.

'Hang on, honey, let's get this clear. First, is your mommy epileptic? Does she have epilepsy, with seizures? Can you tell me?'

'Yes, she has stase-a-lepticus, she goes unconscious…'

'Rip?' she called across the waiting room. 'Getting some information for you here.'

'I'm hearing it, but I wish we had an actual history. She's still seizing. I can't get in there to check her ABCs or the severity of that bump. I wish we had Merril.'

'And Jeannie only knows to press the button for her, not if someone else has something happen to them.' Alice continued.

Jeannie, Jo registered. The dog. But not just the family pet?

'A button Jeannie presses that connects to a service which calls an ambulance for your mommy?' she asked the six-year-old.

'Yes, so Mommy was scared when Jeannie wouldn't go sit because that means a seizure's coming. See, Jeannie always knows first. Sometimes I know because Mommy sighs and makes a noise with her tongue, but not always. And I was in the basement with music on, so I didn't know until Jeannie was barking because she didn't want to let Mommy bring Cody in the stroller, to get here before the seizure.'

'Rip, are you listening to this? Are you following?' Alice

was doing her best, but a clearer explanation was beyond her six-year-old verbal skills. This was getting too complicated.

'Think so,' Rip said. 'OK, she's limp now. I'm going to give her oxygen. She's not wearing a medical alert bracelet.' He spoke rapidly.

'She takes it off when she washes dishes,' Alice offered. 'She forgot to put it back on because of Cody.'

'Dotty, see if you can contact the right company and get them to pull up her details,' Rip said. 'She probably has protocols on file. Some kind of information anyhow. Do we have Mr Grafton's phone number?'

'Yes, in the little girl's file we started yesterday.'

'Call him, too.' He raised his voice and spoke to the waiting patients. 'I'm sorry, everyone. It's obvious we have a slight emergency here. Probably don't need to tell you we'll be running a bit late.'

Jo had already turned her attention back to Alice and Cody, who was still screaming. It must still be only a few minutes since the family had arrived, but it felt like longer.

'Honey, now you must tell me. What happened to Cody?' she asked Alice.

'He pulled the kettle on himself when it was near boiling. It was on the hotplate on the front of the stove and Mommy didn't know Cody could reach that high. I think our stove in the other house was higher. She says she only has to turn her back for a second, now he's a Terrible Two, and he's into everything.'

'So he's burned?' Jo had gotten the safety straps unbuckled at last, having cursed her own fingers. Now she could unwrap the wet, padded quilt and lift Cody out.

Peeling away another wet piece of cloth—a soaked hand-towel—she could see for herself that his chest and shoulders were an angry red, and he was still screaming. Ideally, the burns should be cooled for twenty minutes. At a guess, around half of that time must have passed since Mrs Grafton had covered him in the wet cloth, but it was better to be safe than sorry. And how 'near' to boiling had that kettle been?

A quick but careful look told Jo that the critical areas of Cody's airway, face and hands had been spared contact with the scalding water, but even a mild, partial-thickness burn this extensive would be incredibly painful. No wonder his cries were challenging her eardrums, poor little man. A rough estimate of the burn area gave her a figure of around twenty per cent of the body.

Should she start fluid replacement or leave that to the paramedics? They did have IV equipment here, although it was rarely needed. They also had a small supply of morphine, which Cody definitely needed for the pain...if she could calm him down enough to get in an IV line.

'Trudy, I need IV gear,' she yelled. 'I need morphine, and I need a foil blanket and hot packs. He needs more cooling on the burn, but I'm concerned about hypothermia. Dotty, get the dispatcher back on the phone and give an update, get a second ambulance on the road. I'm going to take him into my treatment room.'

The second ambulance wasn't a luxury. The angry red of Cody's scalded skin jumped out at Jo again as she carried him in her arms. As well as extending over his whole chest, shoulders and part of his arms, it disappeared down below the elasticised waist of his disposable diaper.

Seeing its plastic covering, Jo prayed that the boiling fluid hadn't penetrated as far as the sensitive genital area, where burns could do critical damage. The plastic and padding just might have offered enough protection. She could feel that Cody's navy blue corduroy trousers were wet. From the sodden comforter, or from the kettle water?

Reaching the treatment room, with Alice following, she levered off the toddler's shoes and eased his trousers down. Wet fabric clung to wet skin, and it was hard to do it gently. With a new source of pain, however, Cody screamed so hard that his body stiffened and shuddered in a frightening mimicry of his mother's recent seizure.

'I'm sorry, little man,' Jo murmured. 'I'm trying. I know it hurts. I'm sorry.'

Alice was still speaking. 'And I came up from the basement because Jeannie was barking and Mommy was calling me to come with her. She wanted to run here with Cody in the stroller, because she hasn't had the ambulance here since we came to Harriet, and she didn't know how long it would take, but Jeannie didn't want to let her go, because she always knows first—'

'So Jeannie is trained to take care of your mommy?' Jo asked while she worked on the little boy. 'To warn her and protect her when the seizures come? Cody, honey, I know this hurts. I want to see the burns, sweetheart, and as soon as I can, I'm going to give you something to make the hurting stop.'

Could he even hear above his own noise, poor little guy?

She'd managed to pull the trousers off now, and could see that the scalded area extended from Cody's thighs to his knees, with isolated splashes at his ankles. Ripping the tape that fastened the diaper took only a second. She found more scalded skin extending about an inch below the protection of the plastic and paper wadding, where the boiling water had seeped down but, as she'd fervently hoped, Cody's genital area was undamaged.

First piece of good news.

She quickly wet several strips of gauze and layered them over the burned areas that weren't covered by Nina's dishtowel, to continue the cooling that she hoped would ward off the worst damage. The dish-towel felt too warm, so she soaked it again in colder water and laid it back in place, every movement challenged by Cody's screams and shudders.

'Yes, she's a trained seizure alert dog, and she's ten years old,' Alice was saying, 'and Mommy's had Jeannie since she was two.'

'IV gear, morphine and foil blanket, Dr Middleton,' Trudy said. 'But I'm still heating the hot packs.'

'Gentle heat. Not too much.'

'No, I thought not. But there's some confusion with the ambulance, Dotty says.'

'Confusion, Trudy?' she asked the practice manager as she began to prepare the IV.

'Another call to this area. Dotty's trying to clear it up. Whether it's a hoax or—'

'I hope she gets a clear answer!'

If the ambulance got misdirected or delayed...

'Sort it out, can you? Get Dotty to. We need it, and I need you here, Trudy.'

'Back a.s.a.p., then.'

Jo continued to set up the IV, but Cody's cries were very distressing, fraying her nerves. She was seriously concerned that she just wouldn't be able to get him calm enough to find a vein in such a small, rigid arm.

A case of serious scalding like this one shouldn't be treated at a family practice clinic. They just didn't keep the right equipment, didn't have the practice, didn't have the mindset of staff in a hospital emergency room. She took a deep breath, realised she had no hope of calming the child and decided they'd just have to hold him down by force.

'I'm back,' Trudy said.

'Hold him for me. His legs. He's kicking...'

'He's strong.'

'He's in horrible pain. I have to get him some relief, even if we have to hurt him to do it.' She felt close to tears herself, and made one last attempt to talk to the little boy. 'Cody, honey, we're going to give your arm a little prick, and then put on some tape. Oh, sweetheart, you can't even hear me, can you? Hold him, Trudy.'

She pinned his body against her own, managed to stretch out his arm and got another little piece of good news. He'd been screaming so hard his veins were standing out more prominently than they would have done normally. This one here would work nicely, in the crook of his elbow, if she could keep his arm still...

'Trudy?'

'Doing my best.'

'Keep doing it. Cody, nearly there, sweetheart. We are. I promise.'

He drew a shuddering breath and she seized the moment. She slipped the needle in and got the vein first try, felt a huge wash of relief and worked faster than she'd ever done in her life, getting it safely taped before Cody escaped her imprisoning arms and knocked it out again.

OK, done.

Now, the tubing, the bag, the port for the syringe of morphine. Get his weight right. Do not make a mistake on the dose!

When Rip appeared in the doorway at that moment, her body flooded with relief once again, even though she barely took a moment to look at him. 'Rip, confirm this for me, can you?' She quickly went through the calculation she'd used to arrive at the right dose. Age times two plus eight, giving an approximate weight of twelve kilograms. Morphine at the rate of point zero five milligrams per kilogram. Round it down to a first dose of point five of a milligram.

He nodded. 'That's right. I'll leave it to you now—just wanted to update you. We're still trying to sort out the ambulance, and Mrs Grafton hasn't regained consciousness yet, but her vitals are good. I'm still not totally happy about the bump on her head. Left a message on her husband's machine at work.'

'Swings and roundabouts, good news and bad,' Jo answered. 'Cody, just another tiny minute. Here we go.' She attached the syringe to the port and slid the dose in, watching pain relief begin almost immediately. It would reach its peak effectiveness within a few minutes.

His sobs and shudders ebbed, and Trudy went to get the hot packs. Rip had already disappeared. Jo could focus on getting the little boy comfortable now, and was confident she'd been right to start him on fluids without waiting for the ambulance. She took his temperature, blood pressure and pulse, and was cautiously pleased with what she found.

Valiant little Alice was still speaking. 'You see, a long time ago before I was born, Mommy's seizures got worse,' she said, 'and she had lots of injuries and times in the hospital. She even got mugged in the park when she was unconscious, and she was too scared to go out and Daddy didn't know if he might have to stay home, too, to watch over her, but when she got Jeannie, it was like magic coming out of Aladdin's lamp...'

Ah, OK, Jo registered.

Not Jeannie.

Genie.

'And her whole life turned around and she even felt safe enough to have us, and she had good doctors who said it was OK, and it all went fine, but she's stopping at two.'

Jo smiled. 'That's a lovely story, Alice. Your family tells it a lot, I expect.' She'd recognised some adult phrasing in there. Alice was clearly a little sponge, absorbing everything that went on around her.

'Genie didn't want to let Mommy bring Cody here, but it was good that she did, wasn't it?'

'Wait a minute, Alice. You were in the basement, you said, and your mommy would have been undressing Cody and wrapping him in the cloth and the comforter to cool the burn, but she was afraid a seizure was coming.'

'And she had her bracelet off, and she probably didn't have time to—'

'You said Genie has a button she presses?'

'When she sees Mommy having a seizure.'

'Only then?'

'Yes, and she listens till she hears a signal so she knows the alarm company is going to call the ambulance. If Mommy is outside with Genie, then Genie barks till help comes. I know how to call the ambulance, too, but I was in the basement. Mostly I'm in school and Cody's in day care, because Mommy does work on her computer, but in Harriet we haven't started those yet.'

'Could Genie have pressed the button for an ambulance for Cody?'

'Mommy didn't think she would, because she's trained to press it for Mommy.'

'But maybe she could have pressed it without Mommy seeing? Maybe she could have decided this was another time when she should press it?'

'Maybe. She's cleverer than a person about knowing the seizure's coming even before Mommy's aura. Maybe she was clever about Cody, too.'

'Trudy, can I have you back in here?' Jo called. 'Or Rip?'

Rip appeared. 'Yup?'

She explained her theory about the possible cause of the ambulance mix-up, and then they both heard a siren.

'I'll go out and flag it down,' Rip said, already on his way. 'To make sure it doesn't keep on up the street to the Graftons' house.'

Cody's burn must have received the desirable twenty minutes of cooling by now. Happy that she could remove the wet towelling and the sodden gauze strips, Jo considered cling film. Did they have any on hand here in the practice? The ambulance probably would. She'd leave it to them. Dressing the burns wasn't as much of a priority as pain relief, warming and fluids.

Less than thirty seconds later, two paramedics entered the waiting room. 'Take the child first,' she heard Rip say.

She outlined the treatment she'd already given, as well as the details on Cody's temperature, blood pressure and pulse, and received approving nods. 'We're easy to please,' said one of the men. 'Just as long as we don't have to undo everything someone's done on the spot.'

'Butter on a burn, with the best of intentions.' The other man clicked his tongue and shook his head. He leaned down to Cody, who was quiet and still, his eyelids half-closed. 'Hey, little buddy... Coming on a ride with us? We're going to race your mommy there, OK? Bet we win.'

Out in the waiting room, as the paramedics left with Cody, Dotty said quietly to Jo and Rip, 'I just got a phone call from the dad, and he's on his way.' Nina still hadn't regained consciousness, but she seemed to be stirring now, and had given a little moan.

'And this sounds like our second ambulance,' Rip said, pricking up his ears.

Genie was pricking hers up, too. Seeing that Alice looked a little bewildered and forlorn, Jo crouched down beside the dog and gave her some hearty pats. 'You're a good girl, Genie. You're a beautiful dog.'

'She's part of our family,' Alice said.

'Yes, she is, and did you hear that your daddy's on his way?'

The six-year-old's face cleared. 'Will he take us to the hospital?'

'I expect so. He'll want to see Cody and your mom.'

'And Genie.'

'Yes, he'll want to see Genie, and tell her what a good dog she is.' Jo patted the animal again, and felt something in its armpit that she instinctively and immediately didn't like.

Really didn't like, now that she knew how important Genie was.

Under the guise of a final piece of tactile praise, she felt the place again, and something was definitely there—the kind of lump she would take action on at once if this patient had been human, and hers.

The paramedics from the second ambulance came in while she was still thinking about it.

What do I know about dogs? Is it just a piece of matted hair? No, her coat's too well cared-for, and anyhow that's not how it feels. It's definitely under the skin...

'Cody!' Nina said in a fuzzy voice on her way out the door on a stretcher. 'Where's Cody? And Alice?'

'I'm here, Mommy. I'm waiting for Daddy.'

'Where's Cody?'

Jo walked out beside her and explained. Still in the post-ictal phase of her seizure, Nina's reaction was muted, confused and vague. She looked terribly washed out, and murmured, 'I often vomit right about now, guys, just letting you know.'

'We're on top of stuff like that, Mrs Grafton,' one of the paramedics said.

'Why...the hospital? I don't always—'

'Hit your head. Let's get you in the back here.'

They'd soon departed. In the waiting room, Alice was still waiting patiently for her dad, patting Genie. But not where I patted her, Jo noted to herself. Not where I found that lump. Maybe they don't know...

'I'm going to drop you home, girl,' Andy Grafton told the dog when he'd arrived and scooped his daughter up in a big hug. 'And I am going to get you steak for dinner.'

'Steak, Daddy?'

'For Genie. She's a good girl, isn't she? She's earned it, pressing that button for Cody, even though it got things a little confused.'

He thanked both doctors profusely, and Jo bit her tongue. Now was not the time to talk about a potential challenge to Genie's health, on top of so much else. They had patients piling up, and Alice looked exhausted. 'I'm so hungry, Daddy! I didn't get an afternoon snack.'

'We can do something about that. I have a cereal bar in my car.' He hugged his daughter again, and called the dog to follow them.

Not surprisingly, Rip and Jo both finished late.

Dotty dashed out the door with an apology as soon as she'd sent in Rip's last patient, as she'd promised to babysit for her daughter that night. Jo's talkative elderly lady kept her for ten extra minutes with anecdotes about her family, and needed a gentle lecture about not stopping her medicine just because she felt better or she very soon wouldn't be feeling better any more. It was almost seven by the time they were ready to lock up.

'Seems as if the Grafton family is going to be an interesting addition to our patient load,' Rip drawled to Jo as he waited for his computer to shut down. 'The only one we haven't seen professionally yet is the dad.'

'Who has risen considerably in my estimation now that the bruises I noticed on Mrs Grafton yesterday can be explained by her falls during seizures,' Jo drawled back. 'He seemed like a nice man.'

'You suspected Andy Grafton was the culprit yesterday? You didn't say anything to me about it.'

'I had no evidence. Just the fact that Nina had bruises that weren't all the same age. I knew she'd made an appointment for tomorrow—to alert us to her medical history, as we now know—and I might have followed through with a couple of questions then. One good outcome for this afternoon's drama is that I don't need to now.'

'I suspect she'll be discharged in the morning, as soon as they've ruled out any injuries from her fall. If we were more familiar with her case, and without that bump, we might have sent her home.'

'I do have one other concern about the Graftons, though, Rip.'

'Yes?'

'The dog. Genie. By the way, it's spelt G-e-n-i-e. She's obviously incredibly important to all of them. To Nina most of all, but Alice clearly loves her to death, too. And the thing is, when I was patting her, I noticed a lump.'

'And you want my expertise as a veterinarian, apparently.'

'I want a second opinion, because we're not vets. The lump was discrete and palpable, about the size of a walnut, located in what I'd call her right armpit if she were a person. It didn't seem tender, from Genie's response. If it had been a woman's breast I was palpating, I would have followed up on it then and there.'

'You'd think Nina Grafton would have noticed it herself, though, wouldn't you? Or Alice or Andy.'

'They've been busy with a move from Brattleboro. They have a manic two-year-old. And maybe they do know about it, and it's nothing.'

'Or maybe they don't know, but it's still nothing, and you don't want to add unnecessary worries to an already over-full family schedule.'

'Exactly.'

He thought for a moment, frowning at Jo but not really seeing her. It was a familiar look. She'd seen it a lot since she'd known him, particularly over the past year and a half. She liked it, liked what it said about the way he focused on things. Her stomach kicked. Thank goodness she hadn't followed through on last night's shoulder pat! A more overtly stated rejection on his part would have made both of them feel way more awkward with each other, alone like this.

Why is my heart hurting?

Because it definitely was a rejection, even though it was subtle?

Could I want him this much, when three days ago I didn't know I wanted him at all?

'You have to tell them,' Rip decided. 'You really do. You just don't have enough background data to conclude either that the lump isn't significant or that they already know about it. You're not a vet, but even a family friend would mention something like that.'

'Tell them as a matter of urgency?'

'Call Andy Grafton at home tonight, once he's had a chance to catch his breath. It's simple, Jo. You have a duty to pass the information on. He can decide what to do with it.'

'Let me note down his home number, then, before we lock up.'

'Oh, *we're* locking up tonight?' He raised one eyebrow and tucked in the corners of his mouth. When his cognac brown eyes twinkled at her like that, something warm swelled up in her chest like bread dough and she could hardly breathe. Why hadn't she noticed those twinkling eyes of his years ago?

Because they never used to twinkle for you, Jo, dear, they twinkled for Tara, and then when she left they didn't twinkle at all. If they're twinkling for you now, it doesn't mean the whole world has shifted on its axis.

She laughed at him—a slightly wobbly laugh—and said, 'Message received, loud and clear. I'm sorry I've left it to you so much lately.'

'I'm teasing you, Jo.'

'But you have a point, all the same.'

'We've both...yeah...needed to make some changes.' For the first time that evening Ripley sounded a little awkward, as if the familiar cloak of their professional relationship was slipping off again, to leave them both with a new way of dealing with each other that they hadn't grown used to yet.

Jo practically added up the evidence on her fingers.

So there's the awkwardness, plus the teasing, plus the twinkle...

Her heart stopped aching, and lifted a little.

'Third night in a row we've had a late finish,' Rip went on, a little too quickly. 'Do you want to come via my place and help me deal with that asparagus and cream?'

'Eat it, or cook it?'

'Both, at this stage.'

Don't read anything into it, Jo, she told herself.

'You can call Andy Grafton from my place, too,' Rip suggested. 'I'd like to hear what he says.'

They checked that Dotty had set the answering-machine, then locked up and left, and Jo followed Rip to his place in her own car. Miffy would be spending a second rare evening on her own, but cats didn't get as lonely as dogs, provided their physical wants were catered for, and Miffy's were.

At Rip's, Jo called the Graftons' home number but there was no answer and she guessed that Andy and Alice must still be at the hospital with Nina and Cody. She'd have to try again later.

She imagined Genie sitting patiently in the silent house, hearing the unanswered phone, and her eyes filled with sudden tears. A dog like Genie was an inspiration, and she had no doubt as to the strength of the animal's bond with Nina and her family.

'They have to know about that lump already, don't they?' she muttered, putting down the phone. 'It can't be significant, surely it can't. But Alice said Genie is ten years old. That's canine middle age. Why can't dogs who are as clever and useful as human beings live as long as the people they care for?'

'Talking to yourself?' Rip had appeared in his wide kitchen doorway.

Jo liked his house. It was a very modern interpretation of the traditional log cabin, with lots of varnished golden wood, a wood-burning fan-forced stove, a high-ceilinged open-plan living area and a gallery level featuring three bedrooms and two bathrooms.

Tara was a quilt artist as well as a singer, and even though she'd taken most of her favourite quilts with her, she'd left several gorgeous ones behind. Mounted on dowel rods on the walls or draped over the backs of couches, their bright, clever colours and patterns echoed those of the throw pillows on the couches, softened the expanses of wood and created a cosy, rustic feel.

'Talking to myself,' Jo agreed. 'About Genie. No one was home at the Graftons', so I'll have to try again later. For now, let me help you cook.'

'You can just sit and sip wine and look decorative, if you want.'

'Not very good at looking decorative.'

Fishing, Jo?

Silly, she hadn't meant to try and squeeze a compliment from him, but that was how it had come out.

'You're beautiful,' Rip answered quietly. He didn't look at her, just kept on cutting mushrooms.

She went hot all over.

I asked for it so blatantly. He said it as if he meant it, but I'll never be sure of that, now, ever.

She was so busy chastising herself that she forgot to answer out loud, and Rip didn't say anything more either. Chop, chop, chop went the knife on the wooden cutting board. A dozen halved button mushrooms landed in a metal bowl with a chorus of muted thuds. Still without speaking, Rip went to the walk-in pantry and brought out a dark green bottle, then opened a drawer and found a corkscrew.

'Red, don't you think?' he said at last, holding out the bottle. 'To go with filet mignon?'

'Yes, that would be nice. Tell me what to do, Rip. You mentioned cream?'

'Yes, I got ambitious and decided on chocolate mousse. If I give you the recipe, can you tackle that, while I get everything else going?'

'Of course.'

'Or would you rather sit?'

'No, I'd only feel awkward doing that.'

'Cheese and crackers with the wine, to keep us fortified?'
'Yes, please.'

He shook a box of crackers into a Japanese ceramic bowl, unwrapped a wedge of Dutch Edam and a circle of French Camembert and set them on a cutting board with a knife.

'And maybe some music...' He disappeared into the living room without waiting for agreement from her on this last suggestion, and she suspected he didn't want to risk too much silence.

Think of some safe, suitable conversation topics, Jo, so he doesn't have to tell you you're beautiful again. Eat a cracker and some cheese, too, so your mouth looks busy until you've thought of what to say.

'Tell me more about Shelley,' she said, when he'd filled the air with what sounded like Cajun Klezmer music and returned to the kitchen to toss a green salad.

'Well, she's short,' he said vaguely, 'about five feet two inches...'

Jo laughed and continued for him, 'And she has a mole on her right cheek. I didn't want a police identity parade description, Rip. I meant—'

He wheeled away from the kitchen bench suddenly, and the vagueness had gone. 'Problem is, Jo, you see, I so wanted to kiss you last night, and now I've got you here again and so the exact same issue is coming up and I can't think straight. At all.' An intense energy crackled in his body, and Jo felt its impact like a powerful ocean wave, even though they weren't close enough to touch.

She put down her wine and narrowly escaped coughing up a cracker crumb. She couldn't look at him. She couldn't even move any more, now that the wine was safely on the kitchen table. 'You did want to kiss me? I didn't know. I thought. But then—'

'Yes, I wanted to kiss you! It was killing me,' he said simply.

Look up at him, Jo, she urged herself. He's looking at you, you can feel it like heat. What's his face saying?

She cautiously lifted her gaze, saw a smooth mouth curved slightly, in a helpless sort of smile, and dark eyes that burned and twinkled at the same time. 'Then why didn't you?' she asked. 'Because to be honest, since, uh, we seem to be doing that, it was killing me, too.'

'Lord, Jo, because I was being cautious.'

'Cautious?'

'Taking it slow. Kissing you could change a lot of things. I wanted to work out how I felt about that. Don't you think—?'

She didn't let him finish but put her hands on her hips and grinned and glared at him at the same time. 'Waiting twenty-four hours counts as cautious?'

'Twenty-four of the kind of hours I've just spent, yes.' He almost yelled the words, venting a frustration they both shared. 'Anyhow, it might be more than twenty-four hours, if I don't kiss you.'

'If you don't—? Rip!' She gave a gasp that was nearly a sob. 'Oh, Rip, good grief, after what we've just said to each other, of course you have to kiss me now!'

He didn't need a second invitation.

The distance between them, across the kitchen floor, somehow wasn't there any more. Jo didn't notice it disappear, didn't notice which of them covered the most ground. She reached out her arms, desperately impatient and eager to discover how he would feel, but then at the last moment she waited, for some reason wanting the final impetus to come from him.

He smiled down at her and brought his hands to rest on her shoulders, curving his palms to fit against her, taking it slow as if he needed to make sure at each step that he was doing it right.

You are doing it right, she wanted to tell him. So far, you're doing it perfectly.

'Hi, Jo.'

'Hi.'

'You are beautiful. You didn't say anything just now when I told you that.'

'I know. I'm sorry. You took me by surprise. Thank you.'

'Hey, no need for that.' He squeezed her shoulders, then dipped his head and brushed his forehead lightly against hers.

'OK,' she said.

This felt so new—much newer than it would have felt if they'd only just met, because they weren't simply taking in fresh impressions, they were letting go of old, outdated ones.

This is Rip.

Just Rip.

Ripley Taylor, MD, whose name sits neatly above mine on the brass plaque beside the practice's front door. This is a man who was married to someone else when I met him. This is a man whose marriage I watched fall apart, wondering if Tara was as much to blame for the whole thing as she seemed.

Rip brushed the backs of his fingers against her neck, as if smoothing the way for his mouth, which came next, planted soft and hot on the tender skin just below her ear. She leaned her cheek against his head and smelled the lingering scent of conditioner in his short dark hair, tangy and sweet at the same time.

He pulled his head back a little, and now their cheeks pressed together in a slow caress. The corner of his mouth touched hers, and it felt right, so right and delicious and full of the promise of more. He took her face between his hands, parted his lips and covered her mouth, moving in a deep, seductive rhythm. When she responded, he went deeper, tasting her and ravishing her, making her satisfied and yet still hungry.

With closed eyes, she lost all sense of time and direction, had to anchor herself the right way up by holding his strong, warm body, running her hands down his back and bringing them to rest against the satisfying curve of his backside.

She wasn't ready for him to stop when he did. Opening her eyes, she found him watching her, his hands still softly cupped against her face.

'Was that the whole kiss?' she murmured.

Jo Middleton, what a ridiculous question!

'No, it was only the test run,' he answered seriously, as if the question had been quite reasonable. 'I thought we should do the whole, actual kiss after we've eaten, if we still want to.'

'You think there's a chance we might *not* want to?'

'Not a chance in hell, from my end. But, you know, we're doctors, we have to allow for rare syndromes and worst-case scenarios.'

'The rare syndrome of having a wonderful test kiss and not wanting to repeat it?'

'Hey, give me a break. I've never fantasised about making love to my practice partner before, I'm making up the ground rules as I go.' His voice dropped to a husky whisper. 'Don't you think, Jo? That we should take it in little steps, one at a time? Don't you think this has a horrible potential to blow up in our faces if we make any mistakes?'

No.

Right now she didn't think that at all.

She tried to imagine it and couldn't. She tried to envisage feeling hostile towards Rip, hiding in her office to avoid him, having to negotiate through lawyers to terminate the partnership while her house was on the market because she felt so negative about Rip that she had to leave Harriet and maybe even the whole state of Vermont, the way Tara had done.

But she just couldn't see it. Rip had been in her life for five years, and she couldn't imagine ever wanting him not to be.

So she smiled at him and shrugged and said, 'I guess.' She ran her fingers lightly through his hair, then brushed her mouth across his and whispered, 'One more test kiss, then, Rip, just to be really sure?'

He didn't argue.

CHAPTER SIX

DR BRECK came up for an interview the following Monday. At least, they all referred to it as an interview, but it was more like a conversation between colleagues. Jo warmed to Shelley at once, and the decision was a foregone conclusion on Rip's part and her own.

Shelley seemed fairly confident also. 'We drove up yesterday, and Lloyd is already getting serious about real estate. From our end, I'd definitely like to join the practice, so keep that in mind when you discuss your decision.'

She left to meet Lloyd and baby Hayley for a picnic lunch in their car, while Ripley, Jo, Trudy, Dotty, Merril and Amanda closed up shop for an hour and went to the Harriet Café for a meeting. Nobody voiced any doubts about Dr Breck and everybody agreed that it had been an easy decision on all sides. At her own request, Shelley would start as the new partner in just two weeks' time.

Spring was definitely on the advance today, like a military campaign marching up from the south. The calendar had turned over to April. Down in the Carolinas, the trees might already be starting to show a fuzz of green. That hadn't yet happened here in the colder northern climes of Vermont, but the promise of colour and scent infused the air in some indefinable way that you felt without having the right words for.

Jo talked with Dotty about their garden plans for the summer, and while hostas and impatiens and hybrid tea roses featured in her conversation, her thoughts kept drifting to the delicious, secret memory of kissing Rip four days ago, the way thistledown drifted on warm, sunny air.

She couldn't help watching him across the table more often and more closely than she should, with a little kick of pleasure and anticipation and, yes, possessiveness in her heart. Nice possessiveness, tender and warm and generous.

Could possessiveness be generous? Was that too much of a contradiction? She didn't think so. As he'd said on Thursday night, however, all of this was new. She knew they both had a lot of exploring still to do.

By mutual agreement, they hadn't seen each other over the weekend. Ripley had been on call Friday and Sunday nights, while the other practice in Netherby had taken the hours in between. He must have gone skiing, because he had a tan line cutting across his face, below the paler shapes that showed where his sunglasses had been.

Jo had skied at one time, but after Mamie's stroke she'd fallen out of the habit. Her skis probably had rusted edges and bindings now, since she'd left them almost forgotten in the basement for the past four years. She'd spent the weekend focusing on the coming warmth, not the departing cold, but next winter, she vowed, it might be time to invest in some new equipment.

In case Rip and I...

No. For herself. Because she liked it.

Ripley was eating a bacon, lettuce and tomato sandwich, accompanied by sparkling mineral water and a side order of fries. Poor thing. His mood was fine, thanks to the patch on his arm, but nicotine replacement didn't deal with the whole cigarette habit. The way he picked up his French fries and slid them into his well-shaped mouth, and the way he once or twice patted the breast pocket where he always used to keep his cigarettes, told Jo that he was still finding this tough.

She needed to be patient, she told herself, if he wanted to approach the shift in their relationship more cautiously than she did. And she needed to be brave, in case the shift was temporary and didn't work out.

Thursday's kiss did its thistledown drift into her thoughts again.

Not the test kiss.

The real kiss.

The one they'd had after dinner and wine.

The one when his strong male body had seemed like even more of a treat to have in her arms, and when she'd wanted to find out so much more about what it was like— all the detail that seemed so important and precious in a lover. His body's patterns of hair and soft skin, firm muscle and hard bone, its tenderest places, the way it moved and responded to touch far more intimate than just mouth on mouth, no matter how delectable that was.

Despite her hunger to move forward, she'd told him, 'I do kind of like the idea of taking this slowly,' when they'd agreed to stop at a kiss and part for the evening.

She appreciated what his caution said about him, and realised that Tara might have something to do with it, too. He didn't want to repeat anything that in hindsight seemed like a mistake.

Jo shared this feeling in relation to her own past. Jack had wanted full love-making the same night as their first kiss, and in the grip of a heady crush, she'd given it to him. It hadn't been satisfying for her. Too much, too fast, too soon. It had taken her weeks—months, maybe—to learn how to make their bodies work together so that he wasn't the only one to attain full pleasure.

Rip bit another French fry in half and met Jo's gaze across the table. Their secret smile lasted for just the blink of an eye, but that was enough for now. 'You should have ordered the home fries, Rip,' she teased him. 'They're not such a suggestive shape for an ex-smoker.'

'The suggestive shape was the whole point,' he said. 'That and the salt.'

'Dr Taylor, you've got Don Gregory coming in this afternoon.' Dotty had come in. 'And I know you're going to tell him again to cut down on his salt, so…'

'You're asking me to give up all my weaknesses at once, you cruel woman?'

'Find some other, better weaknesses that don't contradict what you tell your patients is what I'm asking.' She was teasing, too. 'It's spring. Take up a hobby.'

'Might do that,' he agreed, and his eyes met Jo's again.

That kind of a hobby, you're thinking of, Rip?

The kissing me kind?

Yum!

He was coming to her place for dinner tonight. She could hardly believe it was only six days since he'd stormed around to apologise for his nicotine-deprived mood and she'd fed him mushroom and cheese omelette and a glass of wine.

Her favourite season?

Definitely spring!

In theory, Jo's appointment hours finished early on a Monday. Sometimes she stayed late to catch up on paperwork and medical journals. More often, in recent months, the early finish had become stretched right up to her usual going-home time by the extra patients that the practice just hadn't been able to squeeze into her official hours.

Today, she resisted a walk-in who only needed over-the-counter advice from a pharmacist, as well as a fifty-three-year-old who read scary magazine articles on various health topics on a regular basis and invariably developed imaginary cases of myriad ailments as a result. Dotty had learned to get some information from her about the reason for her visit *before* showing her in for an appointment.

Sally Meath's disease of the month today was ovarian cancer. No joke, this one. It was a silent killer that had usually progressed beyond the possibility of treatment before any defining symptoms developed, but as Sally had had a full hysterectomy including ovaries ten years previously, she needed only a thirty-second verbal reassurance that she couldn't possibly have the disease.

'But did you call up that therapist I mentioned to you, Sally?' Jo asked. She'd tried to suggest in the past that Sally should receive some counselling from a trained psychologist. The imaginary symptoms were getting more frequent and less plausible.

'I lost the card.'

'They'll give you another one at the front desk, OK? Put it in the credit-card section of your purse this time maybe. I'll call the therapist myself and tell her you'll be coming in.'

With that, she was able to get away, and it was still only four o'clock. She'd shopped on the weekend. She could leave her car out front, here at the practice, and walk home, since tomorrow's forecast was just as favourable for walking back here in the morning. She would potter around in the kitchen, put on music, put a load of laundry on, and Rip would show up at her front door some time between six and seven.

Ahead of her, going up the street, she saw a familiar figure. Two familiar figures, one of which was a black, woolly-haired dog. 'Mrs Grafton?' she called, and quickened her pace to catch up as the other woman stopped and turned.

'Dr Middleton, hi.' Nina looked tired, but she managed a smile.

'How's Cody?'

'Doing way better than we feared. Or than I feared when it first happened. I panicked totally. But the water wasn't quite on the boil, the burns were only partial thickness and they're healing well. The doctors think he'll be able to come home in a day or two, with some follow-up treatment later on.'

'That's great news!'

'When I woke up after the seizure, I didn't even remember he'd been burned. I just knew I wasn't where I should have been, and he was nowhere to be seen. But I'm always so vague and wrung out afterward. I'm used to finding myself in the hospital without knowing exactly how it all happened, but this time it was a shock that Cody was the patient.'

'I can imagine.'

'We're just grateful the burn isn't as bad as it could have been. If I hadn't been there to get cold water on it so fast… It must have been a crazy afternoon for you at the practice, though.' Nina smiled ruefully.

'Alice was great. She told us most of what we needed to know.'

'And I can't believe that Genie pressed her ambulance button. It's not what she was trained to do. She's only supposed to respond to an actual seizure. But somehow she put two and two together—'

'And confused the dispatcher no end.'

'Hey, don't you criticise my girl!' But Nina was smiling again as she said it.

'Oh, would I, after last Thursday?'

'We'd planned the whole move so carefully, including my coming in for an appointment with you and putting you in touch with my doctor in Brattleboro, telling you everything you needed to know, but then someone got sick at Andy's work and they wanted him to start a week early. He didn't like to say no, because we like to make it clear that my illness doesn't affect his ability to do his job. Then first we had Alice's splinter, and then Cody. I knew from Genie's reactions that I was heading for a seizure and I panicked. Thanks, too, for calling Andy about the lump.'

'Can you give me an update on that, too?' Jo asked. She'd tried the Grafton house again after she and Rip had eaten, and Andy had picked up the phone. She knew he'd been concerned about the dog after she'd told him what she'd found. 'She looks the picture of health.'

Genie was sitting obediently and watchfully beside her mistress.

'Andy took her to the vet Saturday morning. It was a lymphoma, a fatty tumour that's benign.'

'But of course you can't know that until it's been taken out,' Jo confirmed.

'That's right. The vet did the surgery on the spot, and we got the result on the tumour this afternoon, although he'd already told us he was confident about what it was.'

As fast as their own pathology, Jo noted.

'Thank goodness!' Nina was saying. 'Hey, girl, just a couple of stitches in there? Healthy, healthy dog? I'm not going to have to do without you any time soon, am I, Genie-girl?' Nina crouched down and gave her beloved watchdog some hearty pats and a big hug. Genie panted enthusiastically. 'Don't you go getting sick! Don't you go giving your best friend any more scares with horrible lumps, OK?'

'She's a beautiful dog, Mrs Grafton.'

'Please, call me Nina!' the other woman said as she straightened again. 'You look as if you're walking home, so we must live pretty near each other. Please, stop by some time. We have a great deck out back for sitting on when the weather gets warmer. Seriously, do stop by.'

'I will,' Jo promised, and meant it. She hadn't found the opportunity to make the kind of female friends she needed in this town—part of that rut she'd let herself get into and was so determined to climb out of this spring.

Heading on up the hill, her feet and her spirits felt light. Helium balloon light, almost enough to make her dizzy. How long did she have to wait until she'd see Rip? Two hours, three at the most.

It was silly to count the minutes and watch the clock, but Jo did it anyhow, and enjoyed the giddy teenage feeling it gave her. Six o'clock came and she had her laundry done, soup made, wine chilling and the ingredients for a quick pasta sauce cut up and sitting neatly beside the stove in various-sized bowls as if they were waiting to star in a TV cooking show. She didn't expect Rip to arrive on the dot, so she wasn't worried or annoyed, although counting the minutes that elapsed after six wasn't as delicious as counting the ones before.

Rip only left her in doubt for twenty such minutes, and then the phone rang and she heard his voice, pitched at a confidential level. 'Listen, I'm still going to make it,' he said, 'but something's come up.'

'At the practice?'

'No, at home. I can't…uh…' His tone changed. 'There's not much detail on the prognosis at this stage.'

Translation—someone's listening in the background now, and I can't talk freely.

'Are you expecting some results tonight?' Jo asked, playing along while feeling ridiculously close to tears. He didn't sound angry or distant or— But her intuition had gone into overdrive and she knew this wasn't a quick-fix hiccup.

'I'm not very experienced with this kind of surgery,' Rip said.

'Oh, can't we drop this? Why can't you talk?' she asked bluntly.

'Because there are staffing issues…uh…a colleague… Look, it's OK. I'll get there when I can. It's OK. I'll get there.'

'When you tell me it's OK that many times, I know it's not.'

'We'll discuss the prognosis when I have more information.'

Jo gave up on any possibility of a straight, meaningful conversation. 'All right.' She managed to keep her voice upbeat. 'Will you still want dinner?'

'Don't know. Don't wait, though, OK?'

'No?'

'Because I can't guarantee when—'

'All right. I'll see you whenever.'

The trouble with experiencing teenage elation in all its Technicolor glory was that you then experienced a commensurate level of teenage despair when your rosy dream castle came crashing down around your ears.

He said he'd get here, she reminded herself. He didn't say he never wanted to see me again as long as he lived. He's probably had a neighbour with a problem dropping in and wanting to talk.

But she knew in her heart that it wasn't anything like that.

'Do I get the feeling that my timing is off?' Tara asked Rip.

'No, no,' he told her, while distantly observing a feeling inside himself that was akin to being torn in two.

New, he decided. When Tara had left, he hadn't felt like

this. Gutted, yes. Physically wrecked like someone with a terminal dose of flu, but that was different from your basic sensation of getting ripped jaggedly down the middle like a piece of paper.

And, patch or no patch, he was desperate for a cigarette.

'Should I have called, or emailed? Are you turning me away? I've been in the house for ten minutes. You've even taken time out to make a phone call. But you've said nothing about what you want and how you feel. My heart's going like a jackhammer, Rip, I need to hear something from you.'

'We're divorced.'

'Is that your answer?'

'You were the one who left, who told me it was over. I never wanted it.'

'And you're going to keep on punishing me—punishing both of us—for the worst mistake of my life, as if I'm not as sorry as it's possible to be that I made it? You're not even going to give me a chance?'

It was the 'worst mistake of my life' line that did it, that stopped him from showing her the door, because in his darkest moments the previous winter he'd imagined her saying exactly that.

Forgive me, Rip. It was the worst mistake of my life, but that's all it was. A mistake. Can't you forgive me one mistake?

Could he? he wondered now.

Hell of a mistake. More than eighteen months of upheaval and anger and grief. Lawyers, bankers. He'd bought out her share of the house at a generous interpretation of the market rate, which was still stretching him financially because, although comfortably situated when compared to many people, a doctor in family practice in rural Vermont wasn't exactly rich.

He'd submitted to the torture his imagination had put him through, over and over, thinking of her with another man. He'd spent months laying the groundwork in himself for forgiveness, for listening, for taking her into his arms and telling her, 'It doesn't matter. You're back,' because he'd done that before during their marriage, when they'd had a fight about some silly thing and she'd stormed out.

In fact, he'd spent their whole marriage being the rational, grounded one, the one who'd protected them both from the accidental downside of her flamboyant, emotional temperament by keeping his own feelings on an even keel, by being the first to listen, and the first to say, 'It's OK.'

So he told her, 'Of course I'm not turning you away.'

They knew each other pretty well. She was attuned enough to his way of expressing things to understand that he wasn't quite saying, 'Of course I'm taking you back.' Or not yet, anyhow.

She gave a slow burn of a smile, ducked and tilted her head a little, and said almost timidly, 'Hug, then?'

He closed his eyes. 'Yeah, a hug.'

He felt her easing herself against him but didn't look, didn't want to see her big, dark, soulful eyes if they happened to be looking up at him. Her body felt so familiar. Small and supple and firm. A dancer's body, even though she'd never danced, with bony hips and neat, round breasts that would probably stay young and high well into her middle age.

Nothing like Jo.

He eased away from Tara, unable to deal with comparing two women's bodies when one of those women was in his arms but it wasn't the one he'd been thinking about all day. 'Look, as you must have heard from my call just now, I'm supposed to be somewhere. Let's get you settled.'

'In the spare room,' Tara said, not phrasing it as a question.

He was grateful for that, but didn't want to bring the issue out in the open by thanking her for her tact. 'It's clean, and the sheets are fresh,' was all he could say.

'I heard you say not to hold the meal. Can't we talk before you go? Can't I tell you how I'm seeing everything now? And what I think was really going on with the divorce? I know you've always hated the idea of divorce.'

'Didn't our lawyers decide what was really going on with the divorce?'

'Don't be like that.'

'Tara, you show up out of the blue, wanting to *un*-derail nearly two years of our lives, two horrible years of our lives from my end, and I'm the one who's being "like that"? If there's any question of our starting afresh…'

He knew he shouldn't have said it as soon as the words were out. He'd given her something to work with now.

Maybe he'd wanted to.

She was right. He had strong feelings about how important it was to work hard at a marriage.

'Then one thing that has to change is the way we argue!'

'OK, tell me how. I want to listen, Rip.'

'No vague accusations. No "like that" and "you always" and "why can't you ever just". Let's keep it concrete. And rational.'

'Oh, Rip, I barely know what that word means, and you know it.'

'Then maybe you should start to find out.'

'I don't work on rational, I work on emotional, and I think emotion is just as true and real as logic and principles.'

'That's not the point.'

'OK. If you want. I'll try. Rational. Cool-headed. Logical.' She was teasing him, poking fun. Her face had fallen into a parody of sober earnestness. She couldn't hold onto it for long. 'But there's always been an upside to the emotion, don't you think?'

She gave him her doe-eyed smile again, but he wasn't ready to let it melt him.

'I don't think we should talk tonight,' he told her. 'Let me bring your gear upstairs. You don't exactly need to be shown around. There's food in the refrigerator. Make yourself at home.'

'But don't assume that it *is* my home, right?' Her *brave* doe-eyed smile this time.

He hardened his heart. Out of self-protection? 'Assume that you'll be checking into a motel tomorrow. It's just not fair on either of us to try and talk about the past or the future when we're under the same roof. We both need some distance.'

She pressed her lips together, closed her eyes and nodded—conceding, taking it on the chin. He couldn't help suspecting that this was all a performance, and yet he didn't understand why she'd think that necessary.

Surely one thing that had always worked between them was honesty? Blazing, ever-changing honesty on her part, because she didn't believe that honest feelings had to be consistent, but honesty none the less.

Ripley hadn't needed to find her in bed with Trent Serrano to know that she'd been having an affair, for example. She'd told him straight out.

'I'm in love with another man, Rip. I'm sorry. It just happened. I haven't slept with him yet, because I couldn't do that to you.'

Had she wanted a medal for that? he'd wondered later, when the anger had hit.

'But he wants me to go back to Nashville with him and

I can't say no. I want to say no, because I still care about you. So much.' Her voice had dropped to a whisper on those two words. 'But this thing is pulling on me so hard. I never knew it was possible to feel this way. I'm so sorry.'

Now she said, 'Thanks for not sending me to a motel right now, tonight. I guess you're right. We need to take this one step at a time.'

He considered challenging her assumption that there were any steps to take, but that would only launch them into just what he didn't want tonight—a piece by piece picking apart of what had happened in the past and what might be possible in the future, while Jo was waiting for him, not knowing what on earth was going on.

Even as her practice partner, he owed her better than that, and as her lover...

His mind froze, on high alert.

Good grief, had Tara sniffed at the air and sensed the shift in his feelings the way old Mr Liddle sensed the coming of spring? Her timing, as always, seemed expressly designed to extract the biggest emotional roller-coaster ride out of the situation.

Rip wasn't Jo's lover yet.

Would he ever be?

He needed to see her before he totally ruined her evening.

His, he knew, was ruined already.

'So did you eat?' Ripley asked as he prowled into Jo's house, more restless than Miffy on a good hunting night.

'Not yet. I gave you some grace, and you weren't long, so it was fine.'

'You should have eaten.'

'It was fine,' Jo repeated, painfully aware, as she had

been on the phone, that it wasn't remotely fine. 'What's happened, Rip?'

'Tara's here.'

Two words, and Jo's stomach felt like it had dropped twenty feet in less than a second. She didn't need more than two words. Ripley's strained, hollow tone and her own blow-by-blow knowledge of all the painful steps involved in his separation and divorce filled in the rest of the picture—or at the very least suggested possible scenarios.

Tara wasn't back in Harriet for next weekend's antique fair, or to pick up the quilts she'd left behind. She was here to pick up their marriage.

'What are you going to do?'

'I don't know.'

She wanted to call him on that answer. It was a terrible answer! The worst! The only virtue in it was that she knew it must be true, because Rip wouldn't lie or prevaricate to her about something like this.

Her professional colleague Rip wouldn't, at least.

But maybe the new, personal Rip who'd entered her life would.

'Any predictions on when you will know?' she asked, trying not to give the words any barb. 'Any mechanisms for achieving certainty?'

Bzzt! The barb alarm had just sounded. A woman couldn't put that many syllables into five words without sounding sarcastic and desperate.

'I'm sorry,' she added quickly. 'I was just about to offer you an ashtray, but maybe I should be begging you for a cigarette instead.'

'You don't smoke, Jo. You've never smoked.'

'There could be a case for my starting.'

'And neither do I. So, no, I don't have cigarettes.'

'You wish you did, right?'

'Don't joke about this.'

'You prefer the bitchy sarcasm instead?'

'You're not bitchy.'

'No? Lord, I want to be! I'm trying as hard as I can!' She gave a hysterical sort of sob-slash-laugh.

He paced closer to her, right into her space, and her new awareness of him slammed against her body like a blast of furnace-heated air. It practically flattened her lungs. It magnetised her body. It shredded her willpower completely and she reached out to touch him because her fingers just couldn't stay away.

She curved her hand around his upper arm and ducked her head, not quite ploughing it into his chest but waiting for him to pull her against his shoulder. He didn't, even though he didn't make any attempt to move away. They both stood there as if frozen, and Jo felt every pulse in her body beating, centred around an ache of need low in her belly. She wanted the ache, even though it hurt.

'Can we go for a walk?' Rip said at last. 'If you're not going to turf me out the front door—which I wouldn't blame you for, by the way—then could you keep me company and listen while I say things that I probably shouldn't say to you?'

'Oh, Rip, what kind of a question is that?' She looked up at him and found a mouth that looked almost numb. She traced its smooth shape with her fingertips and he kissed them then took her hand away. She felt as if he *owned* her fingers now.

'I mean, hell, Jo, you should be the last person I say them to,' he went on. 'But you're the person I need to say them to, so if you can stand it... You're right, I want a cigarette. I'm not having one. But I'm going to make a full and fair disclosure of my craving—'

'So I'm prepared to duck if necessary?'

'Something like that. It's such a horrible habit.' He still had her wrist imprisoned in the circle of his thumb and forefinger like a handcuff, although it didn't hurt. She wanted to twist her hand so she could lace their fingers together. 'And this is incredibly unfair to you, Jo, I know that.'

'Tara's the one who is being unfair.'

'You think so?'

I'll be able to write a magazine article soon, Jo thought.

How to put off a man who's not sure yet if he's actually in love with you. Step one. Say nasty things about the ex-wife who wants him back.

She stuck to her ground, kept her voice steady. 'Yes. I think she could have phoned, or...not emailed. Written. On a decent card. To ask your permission to come, or at least to tell you she was planning to come. Give you some warning, and a chance to work out how you felt.'

'Maybe she thought I wouldn't know how I felt until I saw her.'

'What do you think, Rip? It's your opinion that counts. Do you think she's being unfair?'

'Let's go for that walk. Seriously. I can't stand here like this.'

She tried not to let him see how much her hand was shaking as she grabbed her keys and jacket and locked the house. It was a still, chilly evening, and their breath began to steam at once, even though it wasn't yet fully dark. Jo hadn't brought a hat or gloves, but jacket pockets and an upturned collar dealt adequately with the problem.

'I hate the timing on this,' Rip said, once their feet had established a rhythm. In Jo's quiet street, they could walk on the road and only occasionally needed to veer to the kerb to avoid a passing car. He hadn't answered the fairness question.

'You mean you wish she'd done this two weeks ago,' Jo said, 'before there was any question of...of something between you and me.'

'That, or the opposite. Months from now when you and I would have had more time.'

Months?

He was expecting to need months to work out how he felt about her?

Somehow that idea struck Jo like a slap in the face, stinging and brutal, and she realised she didn't need months, or days, or hours. She didn't need another second. She loved him, was in love with him, wanted him, needed him. If she sat down with pen and paper, she could probably write a list of all the reasons why, and all the reasons would make sense, but the reasons weren't what counted.

What counted was simply the overwhelming feel of it in her heart, the rightness of it, and the way her heart had already started to kind of *backdate* it, so that she could think of things he'd said or done months ago and they instantly became part of the new way she saw him and felt about him—the way he clearly didn't yet feel about her.

Didn't yet?

Or never would?

'But as it is,' he was saying, 'we're stuck in this limbo. Jo, it's only a year since I would have done almost anything to save my marriage. I believe in marriage as an idea, and I believed in what Tara and I had. I went into it with heart and faith and I hated that it failed. And it's only been for the past month or two that I've felt remotely ready to move forward.'

'You have to move forward, though, don't you?' she said, trying to keep her aching heart out of the equation, so that any advice or opinion she gave him would be fair.

I don't want to be fair, said her heart. *I want to reach out and grab.*

'Even if it's with Tara,' she went on, 'you have to go forward, put the relationship on a new footing. I don't believe that human beings can just go back and start from some arbitrary point where their lives diverged onto the wrong track. We're not freight trains in a shunting yard.'

'That's true. You're right. It would be a new beginning, not a going back. We'd have a lot to talk about, and a lot to work out.'

'A lot to forgive, on your side,' Jo couldn't help saying.

Low blow or act of friendship, to remind him about the other man in Tara's life?

'That, too,' he agreed, his reaction too neutral.

Jo wanted to see him get emotional.

Angry or passionate or sad.

She didn't care which, just something...something for her to grab onto and hold.

'She wanted to talk tonight,' he went on. 'To get it settled and decided, the way people settle on new bathroom tiles. I told her we couldn't do that. We never could have done that.' He shook his head.

'So you'll need some time?'

'Yes. Which is so unfair to you.'

'Tara can't be expected to be fair to me. She doesn't know about me...'

'Unfair of me, I meant.'

'If there's anything to know,' she added.

'What?' he said sharply.

She took a deep breath and a quick look sideways. His face was set in serious lines, emphasising the smooth square cut of his profile with its straight nose and high forehead and strong jaw.

'Is there anything for Tara to know, Rip?' she asked.

'About you and me? We've only just started this. We haven't really started it. We've kissed each other. Once.'

'Twice.'

She didn't remind him that the first one had been just a test. They weren't teasing each other now. 'We haven't slept together,' she pointed out. 'I can just…step away… and—'

'No!'

The vehement word startled them both. They'd reached a side street that ended against the side of the hill, where there were no houses. He stopped walking dead in the centre of the turn-around and pulled on her shoulder until they were face to face, standing very close.

He went on in a softer, more reasonable tone, 'Is that what you think I'm asking you to do? Step away? No!'

'Then tell me what you are asking, can you, please?' She brushed her knuckles along his jaw, stroked his neck, brought her hand to rest on his shoulder. Looking up into his face, she loved everything she saw, and ached for everything she read in his feelings. 'To wait while you choose? To help you choose? Sell myself? Hey, choose me, Rip! Look at my assets!'

He made a strangled sound of disgust. 'I suppose that's how it sounds, isn't it?'

'A bit.'

'That's not how it feels.'

'Tell me how it feels, and how you feel. I mean, we have to do that, or it's hopeless. I don't mind what you say, I just want honesty, even if it doesn't make sense.'

'Honesty? OK, then, let's try. I want you so much, I'm on fire, Jo. I can't sleep. Put your hand on my heart and I swear you'll feel it beating.'

He didn't wait for her to try it, but grabbed her hand from his shoulder and flattened it over his chest, his own palm pressing on top. Was that his heart she felt, or the beat of her own pulses?

'Half the night, I think about you,' he said. 'About your body, wondering how in hell it took me so long to see how beautiful you are, wondering how you'd feel with your legs wrapped around me, how you'd sound when you came in my arms.'

'Oh, Rip...'

'Right now I feel as if I'd turn my back on any chance of renewing my marriage just to find out what we're like together, even if it was for just one night. One hour! If we're as good as I think we'd be, if I could make you...' He stopped.

'Make me what?' she whispered, her mouth close to his, her whole body pressed against him.

'Cry like a baby. Moan and twist and— That's what I'm thinking about. It's not what I should be thinking about. I should be thinking rationally about my whole future, or honourably about what's best for you, but I can't.'

She took a shuddery breath. 'Then don't. I don't mind. I love the idea that you want me so much.'

'Yeah?'

'Yeah, I do, since we're being honest. And...again...since we're being honest, I want you that much, too.'

'Oh, hell,' he muttered. 'Then let's go to bed right now.'

CHAPTER SEVEN

THEY barely talked as they walked back to her place. Rip seemed too overwhelmed by what they'd just said to each other, and that had to be good, didn't it? Jo was overwhelmed herself.

No man had ever spoken that way to her, declared the intensity of his desire for her in such graphic, heartfelt language. The word 'love' had not been mentioned, but she hadn't expected that. Not tonight. Not even if Tara hadn't been waiting at his place.

Jo had to consider Tara, though.

Should I not sleep with him because she's here?

They're divorced.

Will I feel better later on, if they go back to their marriage, and I haven't slept with him?

Or will I feel worse?

As if there's some action I could have taken to tip the balance in my favour and I didn't have the courage?

Is that turning the whole thing into a contest?

She hated the idea of being in competition with Tara for Ripley Taylor's heart, hated the idea of playing this like a game in which he would be her prize if she did everything right, and Tara's prize if she didn't.

It's not like that, said her heart, but she didn't know if her heart was the thing she should trust. Hearts were too often in cahoots with hormones, and she wasn't convinced that hormones could be trusted at all.

They'd begun walking up the path to Jo's front door

before Rip said anything, and even then it wasn't a fluent speech. 'Still OK?'

'Yes.'

'Are we rushing this?'

'Yes, but I don't care. Well, no, on second thoughts, we're not rushing it. We've known each other for five years, Rip. How could we be rushing?'

'You know what I mean.'

'But I think what *I* mean counts, too. We know so much about each other. There's safety in that.'

'And a risk also.'

'Tell me how you see it.'

'That we're rocking a very seaworthy boat.'

'So you've changed your mind?'

He swore, then he laughed. 'No, Jo, I have most definitely not changed my mind.'

She knew it, but she'd been prepared to test him a little. She liked the hot confidence of his answer. Stopping to unlock her front door, she looked up at him over her shoulder and smiled, and he smiled back and they got locked in the smiles and couldn't look away for, oh, a minute at least. Finally she focused on the door again.

Standing just behind her, Rip wrapped his arms around her, letting his hands rest just beneath her breasts. 'Got the wrong key?'

'No...'

'Can't find the slot? Let me help... Is this helping?'

'Kissing my neck?'

'And touching your breasts.'

'Not exactly, but please don't let that stop you.'

'I won't.'

She turned the key in the lock and let the door swing open, but didn't take a step forward. Instead, she leaned back against him, wanting to feel the strength and heat of his body against her back, enjoying the new rights they'd given each other over each other's space.

I can do this, Rip, because I know how much you want me, and because I've told you that I feel the same.

'Cold?' he asked. He slid his hands inside her jacket and cupped her breasts through her sweater and bra. Even with the layers of fabric in between, he must feel how hard and tight her nipples had grown.

'Just cold enough to love how warm you feel.'

'And hungry?'

'Not...uh...thinking about that right now.'

'So what are we waiting for?'

'Just taking it slow.'

'Nope. We're not.' She didn't see it coming. He scooped her up in his arms and carried her into the front hall. Across the threshhold, in fact. She thought about that, but refused to consider it significant. 'I don't want to take it slow,' he said. 'I just want to take you. Upstairs. Now.'

He kicked the front door shut behind him, refused to put her down, carried her directly up the stairs towards her bedroom. She wound her arms tighter around his neck, resting them against the bulk of his shoulders, loving the sight of his face so close.

She discovered things she'd never noticed about him before, and learned them by heart—a tiny sliver of white scar just above one corner of his mouth, the fact that one side of his upper lip was just a fraction fuller than the other, the patterns of dark and light that made his irises such an unusual shade of brown.

He saw the way she was watching his mouth and he read it as an invitation. Jo had no problem with that interpretation. His kiss was deep and hungry and sweetly insistent, and she opened to him and kissed him back with her whole soul. That was how it felt—both giving and taking with everything she had.

'You kiss like a peach,' he whispered, not stopping.

'Do peaches kiss?' She stroked his hair and his jaw and his neck.

'Like eating a juicy peach, so warm. And soft. And sweet. It's hard to stop.'

'So why are you stopping?'

'Just to put you down.'

In the half-dark, he laid her on the bed, pulled off his jacket then in one fluid ripple his sweater and T-shirt. He knew she was watching every movement, and when he emerged from the tangle of fabric he was grinning.

'Keep going, Dr Taylor,' she said.

'Turn around?'

'Then turn back again. I want the full three-sixty-degree view.'

They laughed at each other, at themselves. At everything, really. Just at how good this felt, how unexpected and different and *totally* from left field, and yet so right. He flicked his belt open, but he had his back to her now, so she could only hear, not see. The back view was pretty spectacular. Long, strong legs, two tight, rounded wads of muscle, a rippling spine, shoulders like cross beams.

He kept going with the slow pivot she'd asked him for, and a few seconds later there he was, his body glorious and proud and announcing its readiness. She sat up and lifted her hands to her own clothing, but he slid onto the bed beside her and whispered, 'No. Let me.'

He took it so slowly that she almost begged him to stop and let her finish, get the job done faster, but when his fingers began to touch skin instead of fabric, deliberately teasing her with brushstrokes of exquisite sensation, she bit down on her lower lip and didn't speak.

Slow was good.

Slow could keep going as long as Ripley wanted it to.

'There,' he finally said. 'You said something to me about slow earlier.'

'You said you didn't want to.'

'Changed my mind.'

'All done, then?'

'With that part.'

'So what's next?'

'Do you need to ask?' He told her anyway, dropping his voice low and kissing her ear as he described in uncompromising detail what he planned to do to her. She'd never imagined that mere words could set her on fire that way, especially not words like the ones he'd used—short, blunt ones, full of hard sounds.

Maybe it was the need behind the words.

And the love behind the need.

She loved him desperately as she listened to him, her heart and her body were overflowing and she could easily have cried. Her belly ached and clenched, her skin tingled, her pulses throbbed and she knew how swollen and ready she would feel to him the moment he touched her.

'Please!' she said.

'Now?'

'Mmm. Oh, yes.'

'Or do you still want it slow?'

'You're teasing me!' The words came out on a wail.

He laughed. 'All the way. Because I can tell you like it...'

'I love it.'

'Do you love this...?'

She could only gasp in answer, and anchor his head in place with her splayed hand. When he entered her—how long after this first most intimate contact, she had no idea—

she was so ready she was practically crying. He'd wanted that, she dimly remembered. Or he'd threatened her with it. 'I'll make you cry like a baby.'

Or groan like an animal.

Both.

Oh, both.

Oh, yes.

He was lost now, too. She could feel it in the way he moved, and in the fractured rhythm of his breathing. Clinging to him, she couldn't control the sounds that escaped her, and didn't want to. Her body clenched around him in repeated rippling waves, and in a darkened room everything suddenly seemed even darker. Sight wasn't relevant any more, or hearing, only touch and pressure and taste.

When he surged into her, she bit into his shoulder, sheathing the bite with her swollen mouth but unable to mute her own cries. It seemed so long before they finally lay still, she didn't know or care how long, only that on this new side of that dark, rippling space, everything was different.

She'd loved him before, but somehow it was sealed in place now, making her exultant and giving and vulnerable all at the same time. She wanted to kiss him and murmur silly things, protect him like a child, let him know exactly how much of her heart he held in his hands.

All of it, Rip. All of it.

'May I kiss you?' she whispered.

He laughed. 'You need to ask?'

'Might be interrupting something. Your sleep.'

'I'm not asleep. Just thinking...dreaming.'

'But not asleep.'

'Nope. Thinking more than dreaming, I guess.'

She wanted to say 'I love you' so much. So much. Just

three little words. They filled her chest like a balloon of air and hurt her lungs with their need to escape, but she swallowed them back.

I'm not going to lay that on him. I'm not going to open myself up quite that much. Not yet. Not when Tara's under his roof tonight.

'Nice thoughts?' she said instead. Her voice scratched in her throat.

'Very.'

'You're not going to stay, though, are you?'

'No, I'm not. I can't. Not tonight. Thanks for understanding.'

What makes you think I understand?

And are you saying that understanding is a *good* thing?

She wanted to yell the words at him. *Ripley Taylor, I only understand because you've spelled it out so that it's staring me in the face. I only understand because I've known you before the divorce and all through it and in that long aftermath last year. I don't want there to be this kind of problem between us that I have to 'understand'.*

I don't want problems at all. I just want us to love each other, and have a chance to grow into the new way we're going to be with each other from now on.

But she knew that couldn't happen until he and Tara were finished with each other, and if it turned out to be not an end between them but a new beginning... Sometimes a man—or a woman, for that matter—didn't know what he wanted until he'd tried out both options.

Her heart lurched, giving her a sick feeling in her stomach. Love always contained an element of risk. Coming here to take care of Mamie, she'd grown to love her grandmother even more than she had before, but she'd taken that risk and lived through the sadness of Mamie's death. The Graftons loved Genie, who was already ten years old—

halfway through her life even in a best-case scenario. You simply couldn't love without taking the risk of loss.

But not yet.

I don't want to lose him yet.

Not when this is so new.

And I don't want to lose him to Tara.

Tara was in bed by the time Rip got home—later than he'd intended, at nearly midnight. She must have been asleep. She looked bleary-eyed and her hair was all over the place. Had he woken her? She appeared in the doorway of the spare room just as he was about to pass it on the way to his own room. She was dressed in a floating white nightdress.

'Starting to get worried about you,' she said.

'The practice is on call tonight. Haven't you learned not to rely on my hours?'

She made a face. 'I'd forgotten. So were you called out?'

'We had a couple of phone consults between nine and ten, but nothing major.'

'Hmm.' She nodded and narrowed her eyes for a moment.

'But you've been asleep, by the look of you,' he said.

'I'm not sleeping that well at the moment. I conk out early, but then I wake up again. I'm not going to blame you for it.'

He couldn't think of an answer to that.

'Had a good evening?' she asked.

'Uh, yeah. Yes, it was. Nice.'

Fabulous, in fact.

In the glowing aftermath of their love-making Jo had looked radiant, soft, on fire, cheeky and vulnerable all at the same time. He'd felt so tender about her, and like a complete heel, as if he and Tara were still married and he'd just embarked on a nasty little affair that could only end in someone getting hurt, most probably Jo.

They'd teased each other, standing in her kitchen with wine while she'd tended to the quick-cooking pasta dish for their late meal. He'd dealt quickly and easily with two phone calls from patients, and they'd barely qualified as disruptions. Jo had kissed him whenever she'd felt like it, which had been often, and he loved the way she'd exercised her new rights over his body, supple as a cat, seductive as a courtesan.

The spark of life in her spirit, which he'd taken for granted and barely noticed until so recently, tonight seemed to have fanned into a great, glowing coal that had reflected in her eyes, turned her laugh into a saucy, throaty chuckle and even changed the way she stood and moved.

He could sense her courage, because she was giving him so much, so freely, when he knew he'd promised very little in return. He had hated tearing himself away, staying a good two hours longer than he should have done, and that was why he was standing here at almost midnight with his ex-wife.

Dangerous hour, midnight.

'Rip...' She put her hand on his arm, and he knew what he was meant to do.

The memories of how they'd been together were so strong and so familiar. They jarred with the fresh, unexpected memories of Jo just a few hours before.

'No,' he said. No hesitation, no doubt.

For a moment she looked as if she was going to push. Tara-style pushing. The big eyes, the unerring movements, the naughty-girl smile. He held his breath.

Don't do this.

She must have gotten the message. 'No, well, you're

right, we should talk first. We shouldn't pre-empt or complicate. Even for old times' sake.'

'Definitely not for that.'

She yawned. 'I must try and get back to sleep, but I probably won't now. Not for hours.'

'A mug of warm milk?'

'Yuck!'

'I won't suggest anything stronger.'

'No, because I wouldn't take it. Goodnight, Rip. See you in the morning.'

She turned and smiled at him just before disappearing back into her room, and he wondered if she realised that the chaste white cotton of her nightdress was so thin. The way it half revealed and half concealed her body was far more tantalising than full exposure would have been.

Am I tantalised, then?

He was suddenly too fatigued to have any idea.

'The chest infection seems to have cleared up nicely,' Rip said to Thornton Liddle the next morning. He laid his stethoscope back on the desk and unfastened the blood-pressure cuff from around Mr Liddle's arm. 'And your blood pressure is responding to the medication.'

'Feel strong as an ox,' the old man agreed. 'Nothing wrong with me.'

'How are you going on quitting the cigarettes?'

'Well, I'm cutting down. I'm only smoking thirty a day now, instead of forty. Maybe even twenty-five.'

'That's something. You'll try and get lower, I hope, and then cut them out altogether?'

'Taking it slow. There's nothing wrong with my health. I read where as soon as you quit you start to undo some of the damage, so there's no rush.'

Rip didn't argue the dodgy interpretation. Instead, he

rolled up his sleeve and showed Mr Liddle his own nicotine patch. He planned to step down to a lower dose soon. 'This has been working for me. I can tell you more about it, if you want to try it.'

'A patch? Hmm.' The old man sounded sceptical.

'Take a brochure, and think about it. Meanwhile, let's take a look at your eyes before you go.'

'My eyes are fine.'

'I think it's been a while since we tested them.'

'Went to the eye people—you know, the glasses people. They said I'm OK, no problems.'

Rip didn't think they'd said any such thing, but unfortunately he was powerless to take action, he could only provide advice. Mr Liddle's eyes on their own were probably still borderline safe, but in combination with other factors, he didn't have the reaction time of a younger man. Vermont didn't require older drivers to take a road test at any point, and licences were usually renewed for four years. The decision to stop driving rested with the individual driver, and Mr Liddle obviously still considered himself to be safe behind the wheel. Maybe he was right.

'What does your wife say, Mr Liddle?' Rip asked carefully.

'*Slow down,* mostly.' He laughed at his own humour, then straightened his face. 'No, that's the thing, see. With Mona in the front seat, it's like we've got two pairs of eyes on the road. Couldn't be safer. And I'm not stupid. I don't drive at night or in bad weather unless I have to.'

'That's sensible.' Although Rip still felt uneasy. He gave it one more try. 'The AARP can give you advice on how to monitor your driving safety, too. Are you a member?' The American Association of Retired People was a powerful lobby group for older citizens, and provided many benefits.

'Anything that gets me discounts, I'm a member.' Mr Liddle laughed again.

'Check their website or give them a call. They have driver safety courses for older drivers.'

'I'm fine.'

He stood up, and so did Rip, recognising that advice and coaxing could only go so far. He hated sounding preachy, and he had at least two patients waiting. He'd been a little late in this morning, after making a couple of calls to get Tara into a decent hotel.

He'd known she would want some hard evidence that he was serious about the idea, and her reproachful eyes over the top of a mug of coffee had told him she'd jump at any chance to resist. Had she always been this manipulative and this emotionally ruthless? He didn't think so but, then, maybe she'd never needed to be during their marriage. Had he always made things too easy for her?

Jo would also want some hard evidence, and after last night she had a right to it, but he hadn't seen her yet. She'd already been in her office with a patient when he'd walked through the front door, and you couldn't…or at least he couldn't…just knock on your practice partner's door in a thirty-second grab between patients and announce, 'Thanks for the sex. I've reserved a hotel room for Tara until after we've talked.'

Actually, that was more or less how he did say it, in the end.

They had a busy morning, and apart from a couple of awkward smiles, separated from each other by three computers, two practice managers and a long desk, they barely got a chance to connect. He wanted to ask her along to the Harriet Café for lunch, but if Dotty, Trudy, Merril or Amanda happened to be going there, or indeed any one of several hundred other Harriet residents, they wouldn't be able to talk.

Finally, he accosted her over the sandwiches she was eating at her desk...

'The glamorous life of a doctor,' Jo said, seeing Ripley looking at the untidy sandwich wrap she was using for a plate. It was a self-conscious line, and his entrance had been self-conscious also. She felt a ridiculous need to make this easy for him. 'Sit down, Rip.'

'I won't. I just wanted to say thanks, if that's appropriate.'

Was it?

Jo shrugged and smiled. 'If that's how you feel.'

'I feel good. Very good about last night. Great about last night. Sorry that it happened, because—'

'Great, but sorry. Are we making sense here?'

'No. But we're being honest. The timing wasn't fair to you. It might have been exactly what I needed...I think it was...but it wasn't fair. And I just wanted to let you know that Tara is definitely going to a hotel today. That new resort off the interstate. I'll be meeting her there after work and we're going to talk.'

'Do you know what you're going to say?'

'No. It depends on what she says, I think.'

'Do you still love her, Rip?' That was all Jo really needed to know.

'Love's not something you can just switch off once it gets inconvenient.'

'No. True.'

'But sometimes it changes in nature. The transition has to be difficult. I'm going to stop talking now, because I don't know what I'm saying.'

'Yet,' she suggested.

'Yet,' he agreed.

'Could you let me know...?' She took a breath. Was she just being pathetic here? 'Fairly soon what you and Tara decide?'

He swore. 'Of course, Jo! I'll come round and see you later tonight. As if I'd keep you dangling! As if I'd keep either of us dangling!'

Or Tara?

Jo's stomach crumbled inside her like old cheese, and she knew it would be a long afternoon.

CHAPTER EIGHT

JO FELT as if she was waiting for the results of her examinations in final-year medicine, knowing that they were due to be posted at some point that evening.

She made scrambled egg on toast for dinner then couldn't eat it, sat Miffy on her lap but discovered that a cat made a poor substitute for a man's body, pricked up her ears every time she heard a car then listened seconds later to it swish on up the street while her heart dropped.

Finally, realising that she was getting so tense she'd explode at Rip when he did arrive—if he arrived—she grabbed her coat and hat and flashlight and took herself for a walk. It was a fine, dry night, chilly with a breath of falling dew in hollows and still spots. The lights in the windows of the houses were warm and inviting, but there was something very good and nourishing about tramping up and down the streets on her own.

Harriet was such a nice little town, tucked away in the green lee of the mountains, with a fast-flowing river rushing through its heart. You had the ski fields and the fall colour, the antique stores and quilt stores, the hunting and fishing, the ice-cream factory and Lake Champlain, all within easy driving distance. You had an easy, steady pace of life, with a sense of history and tradition if you wanted to go looking for it.

She liked it here.

She wanted to stay, and had no desire to go back to Connecticut where her sister lived, or to Florida where her parents eventually planned to retire.

But she wanted something more—something at the centre of her life. Yes, the traditional things, a husband and children, and she didn't want to have to go to New York or Boston on an aggressive search for this missing ingredient.

She wanted it simply to unfold.

She wanted it to unfold with Rip.

She didn't want this knife-edge uncertainty and waiting, she wanted...

Rounding a corner back into her own street, she saw Rip's car parked in her driveway, saw him coming down her front steps and her front path, unlocking the car door, sliding into the front seat, starting the engine.

'Rip! Wait!'

He was already backing down the driveway and, with his car windows up, he couldn't hear. She ran like a crazy woman, hoping no one was looking out of those warm, inviting Vermont windows.

'If he doesn't see me and drives away,' she muttered to herself, wild with remorse that she hadn't left a note on the door, and even that she'd gone for a walk at all, 'I'll *die!*'

Then she laughed out loud. Wasn't that just the teensiest bit of an over-reaction?

Yes, but it didn't stop her from feeling it.

'Rip!'

In the street, the red brake lights came on and he stopped. He'd seen her. She slowed, already panting—from panic more than from lack of breath. It was pointless to pretend she hadn't been running after him. As soon as he'd zoomed the car in reverse up the street back into her driveway and had climbed out, she told him, 'I was afraid you wouldn't see me. I'd gone for a walk. Come in.'

'I hated not finding you here. I must have knocked and waited three or four times. I even went round to the back.'

'Well, I am here now.' She wanted to kiss him. At least hug him. But something in his body language warned her not to. Not yet.

'You've talked to Tara tonight?' She led the way into the house.

'We had dinner in the hotel restaurant. She's asked for some time, Jo.'

'Time for what?' She interrupted herself, 'Do you want tea? Something stronger?'

'Tea.' He gave a vague wave, didn't care.

She put the kettle on the stove anyhow, just for something to do with her hands.

'Time to think, mainly. The guy she—Serrano, hell, I still can't say his first name. He seems to have moved on. Tara hadn't realised she was only part of a pattern. He hurt her very much, I think.'

'Shouldn't you regard that as a kind of universal karmic pay-back?' she drawled, the humour edgy and witchy and cynical.

'I'm such a nice guy, I can't,' he drawled in return.

'No. Seriously.'

'No, seriously,' he echoed, mocking both of them. 'I wonder if we're all entitled to one mistake. Tara made hers, and it seems like she's the one who's truly gotten hurt.'

'You weren't hurt? Last year was all my imagination?'

'I was hurt,' he admitted, his voice rough. 'And I was angry. And I'm still angry. But I don't think anger is the power attitude in this situation.'

'You think forgiveness might be?'

'Or my being at least prepared to give her time, which is what she's asked for. A couple of weeks.'

Which sounded like no time at all, until Jo remembered everything that had happened to her own heart in half that interval.

'Here's your tea,' she said.

Their hands touched as she gave him the cup, and that was all they both needed. The wash of awareness swamped them, encircled them, enclosed them in the same space where breathing wasn't possible and where every sense was heightened, every perception more vivid.

Jo looked up into Ripley's face and read the same feelings that she had—need and hunger and a sense of connection and trust so powerful that she couldn't believe he'd be able to let it go, ever. They had a foundation for this. They knew each other. It wasn't some fleeting crush, based on a mistaken understanding about who the other person was.

But, then, Ripley must have felt exactly these things for Tara once.

He leaned towards the bench top and put his tea cup down, and Jo knew he was going to kiss her. 'I swore to myself I wasn't going to do this,' he muttered. 'I just came to talk. I swore to myself I'd be able to keep it at that. We can't do this.'

He did it anyway. Wrapped his arms around her and held her so hard she could have let her legs buckle and she wouldn't have fallen. Kissed her deeply, invading her mouth with a certainty that he was wanted there.

And he was.

Because Jo had no reason in the world to want to push him away.

She touched him possessively, as if by exploring his body, knowing every inch of it, she could store up the memories the way squirrels stored nuts for winter, as if memories could ever be enough. Even as she touched him, she knew that memory could never replace experience and promise. This would be the best she ever had, and only the certainty of having the best over and over again in the future could really satisfy her.

Rip couldn't give her that certainty. Not yet. Maybe never. And whether she kept kissing him or pushed him away, what she risked in the future wouldn't change.

So I may as well have this...

For as long as it could last.

Her body seemed to melt against him with its own heat, her breasts against his chest, his arousal hard yet giving against her lower stomach. She held him in place there with her hands cupped across his backside and didn't care what a brazen message she sent.

Yes, Rip, I want you.

Inside me.

Just like last night.

As close as a man and a woman can get.

She began to let her hips slide from side to side, deliberately stimulating the most sensitive part of him, making the barrier of clothing meaningless between them, showing him her own need. He groaned and kept kissing her, his lips and tongue moving with deep, languorous strokes, his hands cupping her face as if he was afraid she might try to turn her head away.

Oh, can't you feel, Rip? I'll never do that...

He did it.

The sudden sideways twist of his head shocked her—hurt her even, because his jaw jarred against hers and she bit her tongue. 'We have to stop,' he rasped.

'Why?' Her tongue stung sharply and she couldn't soften the blunt question.

'Because I told Tara I wouldn't do this.'

'You told Tara you wouldn't sleep with me?' With effort, she managed not to let him see that she was in pain, and the sting began to ease.

'Not with you,' he said. 'I didn't say your name. Of course I didn't. But she guessed that there was a—that there was the potential for something with someone here in Harriet. A new—'

'She knows you pretty well.'

'She does. And she asked me straight out. "Please, will you not sleep with her until we've had time to work out what's possible?"'

'In those words.'

'In those words.'

'And you said...'

'How could I not give her that, Jo?' He stepped back, balling his fists at his sides. 'It wasn't a lot to ask. If I'm not going to at least give her that, then why am I not sending her packing right away?'

Why *aren't* you sending her packing right away? Jo wanted to ask. How much of a chance are you giving her? More than she deserves, surely!

But not more than their marriage deserved.

That was the problem. Jo hated the idea that this was a contest, but she had to accept that it was, and that it wasn't simply a contest between herself and Tara, but between herself and a marriage. Ripley believed in marriage.

He finished, 'And it made sense.'

'You're going to sleep with her tonight?' It hurt so much to say it, even to think it, and her heart seemed to stop while she waited for his answer, which wasn't long in coming.

'Hell, no! My lord, Jo, is that the kind of honour you think I have? I promised her I wouldn't sleep with you until this whole thing is resolved. It goes without saying that you deserve the same commitment.'

'We did last night.'

'I know now that we shouldn't have.'

She couldn't believe he'd just dismissed it like that, even if he had the best of reasons—that he'd dismissed the connection and closeness, the heady heights of shared and satisfied desire.

Ripley had his sense of honour, and his sense of what marriage should mean. Jo was left with little but the feeling that she'd been wanton and desperate last night and just now. She felt so naked that she actually wanted to cover herself with her hands, as if she'd been standing in the middle of the street without clothes.

'I'm sorry,' Rip said. 'It was wonderful. You know I'm not denying that in any way. I never would. But the timing was wrong. And I was wrong—you weren't, but I was—to let it happen.'

'I'm not a child, Ripley. I don't have to be protected against danger and risk. I let it happen just as much as you did. No. Not *let* it happen, *made* it happen. I'll take my share of the responsibility.'

He looked at her in silence for several long heartbeats, then said quietly, 'Thank you. That's probably more than I deserve. I'll go now.'

'Stay and talk more, if you want. You *can* talk to me, Rip. You don't have to feel that I'm disqualified as a confidante.'

Did she sound pathetic? Clutching at straws?

She'd meant it as a genuine offer, but maybe it hadn't come out that way.

He was shaking his head. 'That's not fair. Not right. I'll go.'

'OK.'

'I'll be working at home in the morning till my patients start coming in at eleven, catching up on a couple of things.'

'I have people scheduled all morning.'

'So you'll be having lunch on the phone at your desk again? Jo, you do that too—'

'Shelley starts in less than two weeks,' she cut in, not wanting a lecture from him, no matter in what kind of caring tone it was delivered.

'That'll give you more time for yourself,' he said, approving.

She felt prickly suddenly, not in a mood to concede. 'No, because I'm planning on insisting that Shelley lets me help her and Lloyd and the baby settle in. I'll be carting boxes and filling bookshelves.'

'I'm sure they'll appreciate it.'

'If they'll let me do it.'

He dropped his voice. 'Really am going now, Jo, OK? It's stupid to inflict this kind of small talk on each other.'

'So go.'

She held herself back, leaning her spine against the hard edge of the kitchen bench top, because she knew that if she didn't, she'd probably hold her arms out to him at the front door and either he'd push her away, which would be bad enough, or he'd relent, and after everything he'd just said, that might be worse. He wouldn't thank her for exploiting the weakness of their shared need for each other.

When he led the way towards the door, she followed at a very safe distance behind him. He reached out and opened it, and had stepped onto the front porch before she let herself close the distance. Even then she clung to the door-handle, using the thick edge of solid old wood as a shield, a protection for both of them.

'See you tomorrow,' he said.

'Yep. 'Night, Rip.'

He paused, took a breath, looked as if he was about to say something else, but then he didn't, he just shook his head and loped down the steps. Jo closed the door and didn't wait to wave him goodnight as he drove away down the street.

When Dotty handed Jo the computer printout showing her patient list for the morning, Tara's name was on it. Tara McKnight. Her maiden name. Jo knew it, because Tara had used it a handful of times over the past few years when she'd had her quilts on show in a local exhibition or had been a featured soloist in the Harriet Episcopal Church's Christmas choir.

The appointment was for ten-thirty, and Jo was running a little late, so she didn't call Tara's name until ten forty-five.

'I was hoping for more time,' Tara said in a low, confidential tone as soon as she'd sat down.

'We'll take as much time as you need,' Jo told her. She struggled to keep her professional manner in place. What could this be about?

'No, but... Isn't Rip due in at eleven? I don't want him to know I've seen you.'

'Is this personal, Tara?' Jo blurted out.

There could only be one reason for that, surely. Tara had guessed that Jo was the new woman in Ripley's life. She immediately felt hot and self-conscious and desperate to be somewhere else. She wasn't ready for this. She knew Rip wasn't. Not ready for this level of complexity, for the decisions and the divided loyalties, the commitment, the endings or the mess.

Tara gave a tinny laugh, unlike her usual rich chuckle. 'It's personal and medical and earth-shattering, and Rip is the last person in the world I want to know about it. Jo, I—I think I could be pregnant.'

'So you're consulting me as a doctor?' Another inelegant question.

'Yes.'

'Right.' Jo took a breath. 'Then that's how we'll proceed.' She smiled to soften the statement, thinking that Tara's announcement raised more questions than it answered.

'Sounds good,' Tara agreed.

She and Jo had never been close in any way, not before her separation from Rip and certainly not after it, in the brief interval before Tara had left town. Sure, when they'd met in passing, they'd stopped to chat. Lots of humour and warmth and interest in each other's lives, but Jo knew it had all been on the surface.

She wanted to keep it that way.

'Have you taken a home pregnancy test?' she asked.

'Not yet.'

'Because they're very accurate now, and can be done at any time of the day. If your main concern today is to confirm your pregnancy, you can pick one up at the pharmacy and go through the steps on your own.' She paused for half a second, but there was no instant look of relief on Tara's face at this suggestion. Jo continued quickly, 'Or, if you'd prefer, we can do one here for you now.'

'I'd prefer that, I think.'

'Do you have any idea how far advanced the pregnancy would be?'

'Oh, not very. I—I'm only a day or two late.' She narrowed her huge eyes a little, and lifted her chin. 'Please, please, do not breathe a word of this to Rip, Jo! Because I have no idea yet what I'm going to do.'

'You're consulting me as a doctor, with every expectation of professional discretion on my part. Of course I won't say anything to Rip!'

'If he sees me here…' She looked very petite with her

body bracketed by the padded arms of the upright chair, almost fragile and not happy.

'If you want, I can make sure that the coast is clear when you're ready to leave,' Jo offered.

'I knew he wasn't coming in till eleven this morning. That's why I made the appointment for ten-thirty.'

'Let me get you organised with a test,' Jo said.

She felt a little confused but, then, she'd never considered that she'd understood Rip's wife very well. Why hadn't Tara taken a test in the privacy of her hotel room? Surely she knew how easy and how readily available they were? Didn't every woman know that now?

Most doctors didn't see a woman for her first prenatal check-up this early in a pregnancy, unless there were preexisting health issues, fertility problems or known risks. The initial consultation at around seven or eight weeks could last for up to an hour. At this practice, Nurse Merril Heath would take a detailed patient history and record figures for blood pressure and weight. Jo or Rip would conduct a physical exam and talk to each patient, often with their husband or partner present, about expectations and concerns. Most women then went for an ultrasound and were thrilled to see their baby's heart beating.

Tara wasn't up to any of that yet, but it was hard to imagine how she could keep a pregnancy secret from Rip for long, if she stayed in Harriet. If she'd wanted safety in this department, she could have gone to the other family practice in Netherby. She must have met both the doctors from there. And, of course, there were specialist obstetricians in the area, too. Burlington was an easy drive, and a doctor there would have guaranteed an even higher level of discretion.

But, then, a woman's ambivalence about her pregnancy didn't always allow her to think and act in the most rational way, and Tara at the best of times had always operated on a heavy dose of impulse and emotion.

Did she want this baby?

It wasn't yet clear.

Was it Trent Serrano's?

Jo did not intend to ask.

Within five minutes she had a result on the pregnancy test and it was positive—very positive, the staining almost purple, showing a reassuringly high level of pregnancy hormone. Tara pressed her lips together and nodded. 'So what's next?'

'Well, you have choices, obviously,' Jo told her carefully. 'If you want to go away and think about it, or talk to a professional...' She paused.

'Oh, I want this baby,' Tara said at once. She blinked a couple of times, her face still hard to read. 'That's not in question. Please, don't think that.'

Again, Jo chose her words with care, sensing that there was a minefield here somewhere, although she couldn't locate it. Rip's ex-wife was saying all the right things. 'Well, then you need to choose what kind of prenatal care and delivery you want, Tara. Many women prefer a specialised obstetrics and gynaecology practice, but when there are no risk factors a family practice like ours is very capable of seeing a woman through a healthy pregnancy and birth experience. You would, of course, get referred to a specialist if there were any complications at any point.'

There.

Well said, Jo.

Nice and neutral, suitably professional, and avoiding any assumptions about where Tara would be and what she would want.

Tara was worrying at her full lower lip. 'It's too much,' she murmured. 'I can't think straight. Let me go away and let it all sit for a couple of days. This has come at me totally out of the blue. Even while we were waiting for a result on the test I was thinking it could all be a drama about nothing.'

'Do go away and think,' was all Jo could say. 'Let me know—or one of our office staff know—if you want more information on obstetricians in the area. You have some time. Another three or four weeks before the initial prenatal check-up.'

'That long?' She frowned. 'OK. Thanks.'

'But I can give you the information booklet we normally give women at their first pre-natal appointment, if you'd like.'

'That would be helpful. And, Jo, if you could take a look and see if Rip's here yet…' She stretched her face in appeal, and then she shivered. 'I just don't want to see him.'

'I want to see you, Jo.'

Rip's voice on the phone, on Friday evening.

Destroying my night, was her first thought, even though that wasn't fair.

Her second thought was, had Tara told him her news?

Jo had invited people over to a meal for the first time in…oh, she didn't want to think about how long it had been. It was going to be a girls' night—all the women from the practice, as well as Nina Grafton and a woman called Sandy Day, who ran the quilting and stained-glass store in the main street.

Jo had met Sandy when she'd taken a short stained-glass-making course just before Mamie had had her stroke, but after the stroke she hadn't made any of the featured stained-glass window-panes she'd planned on for Mamie's house.

And anyhow she'd sort of come to consider that Sandy belonged to Tara a bit in the friendship department, because of the quilt thing. Tara had purchased many of her beautiful fabrics at Sandy's store.

Yesterday after appointment hours, however, Jo had gone into the store to get herself organised about the windowpanes at last—she could definitely see over the rim of the rut now, but didn't think she was quite out of it yet—and she and Sandy had ended up having such a nice talk that she'd issued an invitation for tonight, and Sandy had seemed pleased.

Just as if she wasn't in Rip's ex-wife's friendship camp after all.

Her camp?

My goodness, I have actually *never* liked Tara, have I?

Jo felt uncomfortable about it.

Liking or disliking Tara hadn't been important before. When it came to friendships, enmities and alliances, Jo had never enjoyed getting her hands dirty, the way some people did. When she liked someone, she made friends with them. When she didn't, she didn't make a big deal out of it, she just kept it polite and distant and didn't think about it very much. She didn't bitch about the other person behind his or her back, didn't probe too far into the reasons for her dislike, just got on with her own life.

But now…

She was having six women over to a meal in half an hour, and she really didn't like Tara, she never had, and Tara was pregnant, and Rip was on the phone.

'I'm not free right now,' she told him cautiously.

'I didn't mean now. Oh, I mean, if I'm honest, now that I'm talking to you…' He sighed between his teeth. 'Hell, yes, I'd love to see you this instant, but that's not a good idea, is it? I meant on the weekend. There's still some good snow around. I wondered if you'd like to come skiing.'

'Because we can see each other, but it would be safe and public, in terms of our recent agreement?'

'Yes. Exactly. I'm glad you feel the same.'

I don't feel the same. I just understand how *you* feel.

Tara's appointment on Wednesday morning sat in the foreground of Jo's awareness like a wart on the end of her nose, and she felt a deep, witchy desire to spill the beans, break one of the most important ethical rules in a doctor's professional world, act like Snow White's wicked stepmother and poison Rip's mind with the nice, juicy apple of an idea that Tara only wanted him back because she needed him as a father for a baby that couldn't possibly be his.

The new conflict of interest racked her, the witchy nature of her own thoughts racked her, and she knew how hard it would be to go skiing with Rip on the weekend. Unfortunately, however, the thought of not seeing him at all racked her even more.

'I'd love to come skiing,' she said.

But we won't talk about anything personal, we'll talk about the runs and the lift lines and the snow…

'That's great!' He laughed. 'I'm so glad you said yes! Could you hear me holding my breath?'

'Were you?' Her heart lifted to an absurd height.

'Yes, I was, actually. Tomorrow best for you? Or Sunday?'

Tomorrow means I get to see him sooner. Sunday means I get time to see if any of my equipment still works.

'Tomorrow would be fine.'

I'll rent the gear…

'Pick you up in the morning? Nine?'

'Can't wait.'

And she really felt as if she couldn't.

CHAPTER NINE

For half of the drive up to Stowe in Rip's SUV, Jo forced herself not to ask him if he knew what Tara was doing that day.

Surely he had to know.

Surely the two of them had been seeing each other over the past few days.

What would be the point of this period of thinking and working things out if they kept themselves apart?

She could speculate all she wanted, she finally decided, but she couldn't ask and so she might never know. Or had she lost all sense of proportion? She had no idea if asking about Tara was unreasonable, unforgivable, unfair.

She did know that *not* asking about Tara was by far the best way to ensure that there was no possibility of Tara's pregnancy news making a violent prison break from behind her locked professional lips.

Rip brought up the subject of his ex-wife himself in the end, just a mile or two before the ski-rental place where Jo would pick up some gear. 'While we have a chance, I want to let you know how things are going,' he said.

'Yes?' She didn't need to ask what he meant by 'things'.

'We've been taking it very carefully, having coffee together in the restaurant at her hotel. Last night we had dinner there. She's told me some stuff that makes sense.'

'About your marriage?'

'About why she left. With Serrano. Career frustrations tying in to the stimulation of something new was what it came down to.'

'Career frustrations? Her singing? Would she want you to move away from Harriet, Rip, if—?'

'No, because her focus has changed. That's a plus. It's the only thing that even begins to make a fresh start possible. We both agreed on that.'

'Why the change of priorities?' It was hard to ask questions in a neutral way, when the state of her whole heart depended on his answers.

'She realised that singing was too much of a long shot. Serrano did work hard for her, for a while, trying to get her some contracts as a supporting act for bigger names on tour, getting her songs heard by a couple of music companies, but nothing came of it. I've always thought that her real talent was as a quilt artist, that she was happier and more grounded when she was working on her quilts, and that's what she wants to concentrate on now.'

'Harriet is ideal for that,' Jo agreed. 'Shelley's husband is an artist, too. We'd have quite a colony here.'

'Tara is talking about building a separate studio behind the house. There's space for it, and it would be great for her to have the right space to work in.'

'So you're getting down to practicalities.'

He was silent, having heard the edge in Jo's voice.

Of course.

The edge had been as sharp as a razor.

She hated herself, but hated the situation more. This *wasn't* easy!

'Why are we here, Rip?' She couldn't get her voice above a harsh whisper.

He swung the wheel and bumped into the slushy parking lot in front of the ski-rental place, coming to a crooked halt in a space that had just opened up right in front of the wooden building. People came and went in baggy, colourful gear, lugging skis and snowboards, the lenses of their sunglasses reflecting the bright day. Rip switched off the engine and turned to her, his face tight and his eyes blazing.

'Because I want to be with you,' he said. 'You're the one I want to be with. Today. This moment. You're the one who makes my heart do weird things, and the one I think about in bed at night, and the one who makes me smile because of funny lines of yours that keep coming back into my head.'

'I'm supposed to think those are good things. They are. But I'm hearing a great big "but" coming up like thunder behind the mountains, Rip. If you want to be with me, if there's something real and solid to what we've been feeling, then why is Tara even still in Harriet?'

He closed his eyes, and the urgency drained out of his voice to leave it hollow. 'Yes, there's a but. She's…'

Pregnant. I know. She came to see me about it on Wednesday.

Thank the lord Jo didn't say it!

'The one I had so much invested in,' he said. 'The one who must have made my heart do weird things, too, a long time ago, although I'm having trouble remembering how it felt, because this whole situation is so impossible.'

'It is, isn't it?' she agreed.

He barely heard her. 'No, I do remember being giddy with love, living on air, thinking I was insanely lucky, thinking I'd discovered the secrets of the universe. I was twenty-four when we met.' He shook his head. 'And then you get over that, and you learn each other's faults, and you anticipate each other's moods, and you forgive a lot, and that's part of it, part of what makes marriage great.'

'Is it?'

'Yes, the fact that it's the whole…oh…the whole carton of milk, not just the cream on top.'

'Well, I like the image…'

'If marriage was easy, Jo, what would be the point?' He spoke with a level of urgency and emotion that meant she couldn't doubt his sincerity, or the extent to which he was questing for the right answers. 'Nobody's perfect.'

'Of course not.'

'It happens in every marriage. You have to love the other person with their faults, because of their faults. A happy marriage isn't about some fairy-tale ideal of blind bliss. I really believe that. I've always believed it.'

'Your parents' marriages...' she began, and realised all over again just how well she did know him.

She'd always thought they'd had little to do with each other's personal lives, but in fact far more had filtered through over the years than she'd consciously known. Little snippets here and there. A frown when he made some passing reference. A phone call that had him looking thoughtful, or angry. In five years, it added up.

She knew a lot about his feelings towards his parents, for example.

'Yes, they've been a big influence,' he said.

'Tell me, because you don't talk about it much.'

'After their divorce—'

'You were how old?'

'Only three.'

'And you went with your mom, I know.'

'At first, but later, when I got older—around nine—I wanted to live with Dad, and to her credit Mom let me go, although I know that wasn't easy for her.'

'So your dad, after the divorce...' Jo prompted.

'Dad found Julia a couple of years later, and they've been together ever since. Thirty years now. They've had problems. My stepbrother—he's six years older than me—has given them a lot of heartache, taking so long to decide what he wanted from life, but Dad has been with Julia every step of the way. Whereas my mother's on her fourth marriage now.'

'Fourth? I thought it was only three.'

He shrugged and turned his mouth upside down. It wasn't really a smile.

'I didn't announce the latest,' he said. 'It was six months ago. She only told me after the event, so I couldn't have gone, but I met him over Christmas. Anyhow, there's no reason to think this one will last any longer than the others. She'll bail out, if not at the first hurdle then definitely by the second or third. She's not good at confrontation, and she's not good at compromise. I don't want to look back on my life and realise I've ended up doing the same thing.'

'So what are you saying, Rip?'

'I think there may be some new place we could get to, Tara and I, if we tried. She believes there is. She's being very un-Tara-like at the moment, actually. She's not pushing. She's just asking for a chance. And the decision I have to make is whether I want to try and get to that place she believes in. The place *I* believe in, too, when I think about Mom and Dad.'

Jo swallowed a great, painful lump of complex emotions. 'So the skiing is for comparison purposes? Do you ski with Tara tomorrow?'

Another tense silence.

She blurted out, 'Oh, lord, I'm sorry, Rip, but I can't—'

'I shouldn't have called you last night,' he cut in.

Neither of them had made a move to leave the car.

'Not for comparison purposes,' he said, his tone forceful. 'It didn't feel like that when I suggested it. It doesn't feel like that now.'

'Then how does it feel?'

He shook his head. 'This is going to sound— But I'm

going to say it anyhow. It feels like I've been let out of school, and I can't believe my luck.'

'Married men feel like that all the time when they're having an affair, I imagine.'

'I imagine so, too. Jo, we've known each other long enough that I can't pretend my motives are more honourable than they really are, or that I'm more in control of my own feelings than I really am. I'm groping around in the dark.'

'You do have a good sense of honour, Rip. I'm being honest with you, too. This is *horrible*. All of this. I'm thinking that if you hadn't given up smoking ten days ago, you wouldn't have come round that night to apologise, we wouldn't have spent that nice evening, our feelings might never have shifted.'

She couldn't even imagine it. Surely she'd felt like this about Rip since the dawn of time?

'Jo—'

'Tara would have come back,' she went on. 'You would have forgiven her. This would be easy for all of us. Happy endings wall to wall.'

Really, though? Even with Tara's pregnancy?

Jo wondered...

She hated being in possession of this crucial piece of knowledge that Rip clearly didn't yet have. It burned in her, splitting her in two. There was no decision to be made. She couldn't tell him. It was an issue of patient confidentiality that was enshrined in law. But she wasn't only a doctor, she was a woman in love, and Tara was conning Rip, tricking him, she was sure of it.

Will she get a commitment from him, and only then tell him about the baby?

Or was Jo being a witch with a poisoned apple again? Was Tara just lost and scared and stumbling through all of this, Snow White in the forest—she *looked* like Snow White, for goodness' sake!—unaware that she was handling it all wrong?

'Shall we go home?' Rip asked in a voice as wooden as the pine walls of the ski rental. 'Is this going to be impossible?'

Sometimes you just have to be brave when you're in love.

You have to trust, not run.

Rip's mother had always run, and Rip had hated that.

'No,' Jo answered firmly. 'It's not going to be impossible. It's going to be great. The sun is shining, the snow's still deep and dry, high up. We're not setting ourselves some huge goal here. We're just going to have a good day.'

She opened the car door and headed into the ski-rental place, certain that in this, at least, she was doing the right thing.

They skied until the snow became blue with lengthening shadow and the lifts began to close. Jo was rusty at first, but then it all came back and she could match Rip for speed if not for style on the harder slopes.

When he went ahead of her, he waited at the next ridge or chute, and sometimes she made him wait longer than necessary because she didn't start off down the run directly after him but watched him for a while, reading his exhilaration in the way he moved, loving the evidence of how fit and capable his body was, how much he valued the pleasure of using it like this.

Sometimes they matched each other's pace and skidded into the lift line within a few seconds of each other, breathless and grinning, with sun-warmed cheeks and cold lungs. Once, going incredibly fast, he caught an edge and took a fall, tumbling and sliding, with one ski detached and left behind him in the snow. Jo sideslipped until she reached it then carried it down to him, saw that he'd come up smiling though covered in snow, and laughed at him.

They stopped for lunch at one o'clock—hot dogs with ketchup and mustard, and hot chocolate with marshmallows drowning in the sweet foam on top. Even while they ate and drank, they didn't talk about anything personal, only about the morning's skiing and which runs they'd try in the afternoon.

Jo's hair got messy and even her factor 45 sunscreen couldn't quite keep the windburn at bay. Her legs ached, and that little twinge in her left shoulder would probably turn out to be a strained muscle tomorrow, but she didn't care. Nothing was going to stop this day from being perfect.

By the time they'd returned the rental equipment and driven back to Harriet, with Rip's skis still dripping melted snow in the ski rack on the roof of the SUV, it was almost dark. Near the end of the drive, Jo spent several minutes wondering if Rip would suggest dinner together, followed by several more during which she waited for him to break the news that he had the usual obligation to Tara.

Finally, she decided to be generous and said to him, 'Are you meeting Tara at a particular time tonight?'

She didn't miss the slightly startled look he shot in her direction. Startled and appreciative? 'No, but I did tell her we'd see each other for dinner,' he said.

'It's not that late.'

'No, she'll be fine about it.'

'What did you tell her about today?'

'Just that I was busy. Part of the agreement. She can't ask for more detail than I want to give.'

'So she doesn't know that you and I were...' Jo stopped. 'It does feel like an affair, Rip. I've never imagined myself in a situation like this. Sneaking around, talking about this significant other *she*.'

'I know. And I know you don't like it, and I don't either. If you want us to stop seeing each other, you and me, even in the limited way that we've seen each other these past few days, I have no right to ask for anything else.'

Crunch time.

Jo picked her way carefully through her answer, like picking her way through a prickly patch of grass in bare feet.

'I loved today,' she said. 'Because it was simple. I'm not sure what other ways we can find right now that would be as simple. I don't want…oh…cosy evenings at my place, or expensive dinners for two. Dangerous, don't you think?'

He whooshed out a breath. 'Oh, yeah!'

She took a slightly shuddery breath, thinking about the other night and how good it had been, how right their bodies had felt together. 'So I'm wondering if it is best to stop. Now, while we're ahead. Before we make a mistake we'll regret.'

'Sleeping together again?'

'That would be a mistake—' a heavenly, hellish mistake, '—if you and Tara do end up…'

'Yes.' He closed his eyes. 'Yes, it would. But if we could think of something else like what we did today, something public and fun and…*simple,* you said, that was a good word, then we could spend a bit of time together.'

She managed a laugh. 'I'll await your suggestions.'

He didn't take long to think about it. 'How long since you've toured the ice-cream factory?'

'Wha-a-at?'

'Seriously, have you ever?'

'I took Mamie there, just after I first moved to Harriet.

We had a ball. I always meant to take her again, but we somehow never managed it.'

'Busy tomorrow afternoon? I'll pick you up and we'll go for ice cream. Simple. Just the tour and the ice cream and home. Tara is doing the antique fair with a friend.'

'This is crazy!'

'It is. Make it the last thing? Last time we spend together? I can't let go of this yet, Jo. Let's spend a bit more time together. Even just for the sake of making things easier in the practice later on. Even just as friends. I'm not going to let our relationship go sour, even if that means the ultimate sacrifice of eating ice cream.'

He knew how much she liked the stuff.

'Mamie's last meal was ice cream,' Jo said. 'Strawberry. I fed it to her when she couldn't hold a spoon or take solid food. She had her eyes closed, and she couldn't speak any more, but she opened her mouth ready for the next spoonful, until it was all gone. I'll always hold onto that memory and feel glad about it, that she had such a sweet, satisfying treat right at the end. She had another stroke during the night, and— You know all of that. I've probably told you the ice-cream story before, too.'

'That's OK. It's a good story. I can't imagine a better last meal than strawberry ice cream, either.'

He was looking at her, with those eyes like glasses of brandy, drunk neat with no ice. Even in the dark, they were such warm eyes, with little creases in the lids above them that she'd been wanting to kiss lately every time she saw them.

Could she kiss them now? Could she kiss his mouth, with its firm, smooth lips? Or even just his forehead? Kiss the frown away? Taste his skin there, because it tasted just as much like him as any other more intimate spot...

No.

His face wasn't quite saying no, yet, even though it should be. She saw him look at her mouth, the way she'd just looked at his. The connection and instinct and understanding between them was something that must have existed between a man and a woman since before language was invented. Their bodies were like magnets, like puzzle pieces cut to a precise fit.

'Don't,' she told him. 'Not after everything we've talked about. Just tell me what time you're going to pick me up for ice cream.'

'Two o'clock? I'm picking it out of the air. Any time.'

'Two will be fine.'

She would spend the morning getting to work on her stained glass, hunting up her equipment and her book and her notes from Sandy's course, working out what she needed to buy. She would make it seem important by sheer force of will.

Just the way, by sheer force of will, they weren't going to kiss each other here in the dark interior of the SUV.

Rip had lost that hungry look now, lost the softness from around his mouth and the heat from his eyes. He was back in control. 'I'll see you then.'

She only nodded, because she couldn't find any words, and climbed quickly out of the vehicle.

The ice cream was just as good as the skiing.

'We obviously have a similar degree of enthusiasm when it comes to cold things,' Rip said as they sat at the picnic tables in the grounds of the factory, eating from cardboard cups piled high with three different flavours.

'Handy, since we live in Vermont,' Jo said, getting ready to spoon into her mouth a sample of all three of her chosen flavours at once. Cappuccino, strawberry, in honour of

Mamie, and Swiss chocolate almond. 'Vermont has very good cold things.'

Rip had picked coconut, cherry and something that appeared to offer at least three different forms of chocolate in the one flavour. 'Since I'm guessing there might be a shortage of the stuff after that production-line glitch we saw.'

One of the freshly filled cartons of double chocolate chip cookie dough ice cream had got caught in the machinery, causing a major ice-cream pile-up, and mass chocolate-flavoured casualties squishing against rollers, toppling over the side and melting on the floor. The spill had reached dire proportions before the production-line staff had noticed, despite the tour group frantically attempting to get their attention by banging on the glass of the viewing gallery above.

'Glitch?' Jo said. 'It was practically a national emergency. Did you see that little boy in tears?'

'He won those bumper stickers later, and I think the free cone cheered him up, too.'

'You know I think it does taste better here on the spot.'

'The tour was pretty inspirational, I admit.'

'Mmm, and the sun's so good on my back.'

'But you have a coffee-flavoured drip on your chin.' Rip leaned across and wiped it off with the corner of a paper napkin, and all the stuff from last night in his car was back in the air again. The pull. The understanding. The heat. The impossible timing.

He seemed to feel it, too.

He sat back as soon as he'd dealt with the drip of ice cream, and when both their cups were empty, he stood up right away.

'Do you need to get back?' Jo asked him stupidly, thinking of Tara and a possible rendezvous.

'I need to be on my own, I think. Just being in your company is...even casually like this, the way we might have done if we were still just colleagues... It's not fair. To anyone. Least of all to you.'

'I've enjoyed it, Rip. And I enjoyed yesterday.'

'That's not the point.' He seemed angry suddenly—edgy and impatient.

With himself, Jo suspected.

And for once she wasn't going to blame his quest to give up smoking, even though he was now up to a record twelve days. She knew how much he hated to make a mess of things. He was a perfectionist in certain areas, and nothing much in his personal life was perfect at the moment.

'Are you seeing Tara tonight?' she asked.

'I'm supposed to. I'm going to cancel. You were right yesterday, when you talked about making comparisons. That's not what I thought I was doing. It's *not* what I'm doing. I just need some time on my own to think.'

She nodded. 'Of course you do. Take me home, and I'll see you at the practice in the morning.'

Rip dropped Jo at the front of her house. He didn't even turn off the engine, and was deeply grateful, as usual, for how much she understood. She didn't invite him in or prolong their goodbye in any way.

He drove out of Harriet along the Interstate a few miles and then off at the next exit, which led to the resort town where Tara had chosen her hotel. Cruising through the parking lot, he couldn't see her car. She must still be at the antiques fair with her friend Bree.

Fine.

Better, really.

He'd leave a message on the voicemail in her room to say he couldn't see her tonight. He'd begun to find their evenings together a serious strain. She'd been urging him, 'I don't want you to make a decision yet, Rip. I'm not asking for that.' And it had begun to feel like some kind of stalling to him, even though she was presenting it as something they needed—that he needed in particular.

Time.

Time to think.

He wasn't buying it any more. She'd always had the capacity to be manipulative when she thought she needed to be. He'd known that about her from early on. Of course he had. He wasn't an idiot, and he trusted his own perceptions about people.

But he'd felt that knowing it gave him an armour against it. He'd called her on it sometimes, and she'd admitted to it, and the admission had usually pushed them onto a level of honesty that worked better for him. For them both, he thought.

But he discovered as he drove home that he'd lost patience with the preliminary emotional game-playing. Why couldn't they get to the honesty without jumping through all those hoops on the way?

Cut to the chase, Tara.

There's something else going on, and I need to know what it is before we go any further.

He called her hotel room as soon as he got in the door of his house, but wasn't surprised that she didn't pick up. 'I have to cancel dinner, but call me back as soon as you get this,' he told her. 'I want to talk. Not in person. The phone will do fine. But I want to talk tonight. Late isn't a problem. I'll wait up.'

Hours passed, however, and the phone didn't ring.

CHAPTER TEN

BY TEN-THIRTY, when he would otherwise have been heading to bed in advance of a six-in-the-morning alarm, Rip began to get seriously concerned. Surely Tara must be back in her hotel room by now? His message had been firm and unequivocal.

Call me.

And she hadn't.

Could something have gone wrong?

He'd worked in a hospital emergency department in the past, and he never made the classic mistake of thinking, It couldn't happen to me. On certain terrible occasions, the reason why someone you cared about didn't call you back was because they couldn't.

They were frantically arranging flights to get across the country to a dying parent before the end came. They were unconscious in the OR. Their car had plunged through a highway barrier down a hair-raising slope, where no one would find it until morning.

By eleven, the silence of the phone had gotten to him, and he couldn't stand the inaction any longer. He grabbed keys and jacket and got in his car. He'd check the parking lot at Tara's hotel first, and then if she wasn't there…

If she wasn't there, then what?

Call the local hospitals?

Search the highway verges and lay-overs?

Was that why he'd chosen the SUV?

Ridiculous. He was hardly likely to be going off-road, and conditions weren't icy tonight. If she really was missing, he'd need to get the emergency services to instigate a proper search.

The question turned out to be academic anyhow. Repeating his earlier cruise through the hotel parking lot, he found Tara's car almost at once, parked near the far entrance closest to her room, which was locked after hours.

He knew why she hadn't called. It was a stunt she'd pulled before when she wanted to remind him of how much he cared about her. She would have checked her messages—she'd always bordered on obsessive about that, couldn't stand the thought of missing an important call. She might have been piqued that he'd cancelled dinner. And she would have heard the terse impatience and command in his instruction to call back, and she'd reacted against it.

We'll just see if I'll call you right back, Ripley Taylor, after you've cancelled dinner with me.

We'll see what's really important to you.

Yeah, OK, so maybe he shouldn't have sounded so peremptory, maybe he should have gritted his teeth and gone ahead with dinner as planned, but he hated the combative approach she always used. Couldn't she have called back and covered the contentious issue of his peremptory tone and him standing her up via a civilised conversation?

He sat with the SUV idling behind her vehicle for several minutes. Should he go in and confront her, generate an argument that would hopefully lead to a deeper resolution? Or should he call her bluff and go home and to bed?

In the end, when he drove away, his decision wasn't about either of those things.

'I'm worried, Jo. I've been having some bleeding,' Tara said.

She'd appeared on Jo's appointment list again that morning, the last patient before lunch and not one Jo was keen to see. Tara, of course, had no idea what raw nerves she was chafing by her visit. She looked pale and dry-lipped and anxious, as well she might be if the bleeding was serious. Her pale, baggy sweater didn't lend her face any colour and emphasised her petite build.

'Most women panic when they see bleeding during pregnancy,' Jo said, struggling to find a manner that was both professional and gentle. She'd been dreading this visit all morning. 'But it often means nothing. Is it heavy?'

'Not at the moment...'

'But it was?'

Tara frowned. 'There was, um, yes, more of it during the night.'

'Any pain or cramping?'

'Um, yes, some, I think.' Her manner was odd. 'Would that mean something?'

'It can mean the start of a miscarriage. Let me give you a check, and I may send you for an ultrasound, too, depending on how everything seems.'

Jo sent Tara through into the treatment room, where a clean sheet covered the examination table and where Tara could unfold a second sheet to drape over her lower body once she'd removed her stretch jeans, shoes and underwear. Jo washed and gloved her hands, trying to get her feelings back onto an even, professional keel. Tara was ready and waiting just a minute later.

The physical exam didn't take long. Jo laid one hand over Tara's lower stomach, where the expanding uterus would be, while using her other hand to check the cervix. It was thick and tightly closed. She took in a breath, ready to tell Tara that this was good news, but then the significance of what else she was feeling struck her.

This wasn't the orange-sized uterus of a woman who was only around five weeks pregnant. It was way bigger than that—the size she'd have expected at the end of the first trimester, just at the point where the web of muscles across the lower abdomen began to loosen and a woman found that her clothes no longer fit quite the way they used to.

Jo slid her hands from beneath the sheet, and saw only a tiny smear of old blood on her glove—less than she would have expected, given what Tara had said about bleeding during the night.

Tossing the gloves in the bin, she told Tara, 'Everything's looking good. Very good. Almost no bleeding, and your cervix hasn't opened. Are you having any cramping at the moment?'

'No, I'm OK right now.'

'I'll check your breasts, too…'

She gave the kind of manual exam she did when checking for suspicious lumps, and found breasts which again suggested a more advanced state of pregnancy than Rip's ex-wife had estimated. 'Are you sure of your dates, Tara?'

'Oh. Why do you ask? Yes, I am.'

'Because your uterus is bigger than I would have expected. I'm wondering if you could be further along than you think.'

There was a tiny silence, then Tara said, 'Or having twins!'

'That's possible,' Jo agreed cautiously.

'But you don't think so.' She sounded a bit uncomfortable, a bit impatient.

Jo couldn't read her very well, and felt uncomfortable, too. Usually, a pregnant woman's emotions were pretty simple—wildly changeable, but simple. Tara's layered attitude seemed strange, and didn't help Jo to relax with a patient she hadn't wanted to see in the first place.

'I think it's more likely that your dates are wrong,' she said carefully. 'You've been having some bleeding. Could you have mistaken bleeding around four and eight weeks ago as a period?'

'Is that the explanation? Is that why I've been feeling so horrible? I'm more pregnant than I thought.' Abruptly, she covered her face with her hands. 'That's even harder to deal with. Can I ask you again, Jo? Please, please, don't tell Rip!' Tara looked full into Jo's face, her big, dark eyes intense and beseeching. 'Even if there's a medical reason for it, because he's a colleague. I just cannot have him know about this!'

'Won't he have to, eventually, if you're staying in Harriet?' Jo answered gently. 'You'll start to show soon.'

'I need to think. I'm not sure if I am staying in Harriet, to be honest. That depends on… Well, Rip and I are talking about it. Are we done now? Is there any treatment I need…or anything?'

'Just take it easy, that's all. Rest as much as you can. At three months, the most usual danger period for miscarriage is past, and after checking you out I'm not too concerned. But it never hurts to take things easy. And I'm going to send you for an ultrasound to confirm your dates, so I'll give you the paperwork for that.'

She stepped back into her office, printed it off and gave it to Tara.

'Thanks. I'll be in the café. Can you tell him that? If he needs to see me?'

'He still has a patient or two…'

'Right. So tell him where I am, but please don't let him know that this was another professional visit. I'm not sure about your ethical obligations to a colleague, but…'

'Of course I won't say anything,' Jo said, feeling uncomfortable about Tara's insistence and about her narrowed eyes fixed on Jo's face.

'No, I'm sure you won't,' Tara murmured, after a moment. She controlled a sigh.

'I'll leave you to get dressed now,' Jo said, knowing she sounded awkward and not like a doctor with years of experience. 'And you can take this other door back to the waiting room whenever you're ready.' She indicated the second door that opened from the treatment room, and Tara looked at it, narrowing her eyes even more.

'I never used to come in here much. Rip has his own treatment room, does he?'

'Yes, the mirror image of this one, opening from his office, with another door back to the waiting room.' Jo guessed that Tara was once again concerned about the possibility of meeting up with him on her way out.

'Thanks, Jo,' she said vaguely, still looking at the door. It wasn't fully soundproofed, and they could both hear Trudy talking on the phone at the front desk.

'You're welcome.' Jo went back into her office and closed the door to give Tara some privacy.

'Although maybe the privacy is more for me,' she murmured to herself.

She'd found this visit from Rip's ex-wife even more unsettling than her first one last week. First the possibility of miscarriage, then the fact that the pregnancy could well be significantly more advanced than Tara had apparently known. Most of all, of course, the conflict of interest, underlined by Tara's repeated urging to her not to tell Rip.

Be honest, Jo, dear, is it the conflict of interest?

Sitting at her desk, she echoed Tara's earlier gesture and hid her face in her hands.

No, it's just the conflict.

This was an elemental contest between herself and Tara over which woman Rip would choose, and even though she hated to think of it in those terms, Jo couldn't help fearing that Tara held all the cards. The baby wasn't Rip's, but when he knew about it—as he'd surely have to soon, despite all Tara's attempts at subterfuge—wouldn't he do the honourable thing and step in to be a father to Tara's child?

She felt miserable, tense, claustrophobic. Her lunch-break was due, but the thought of sitting here with the packed lunch she'd made this morning, or going along to the café where Tara would also be…

No. I'll go home.

She stood up, went to the door and then heard Tara out in the waiting room. 'Rip, hi!'

His reply was just as clear. 'I still have a patient, Tara…'

'I'm not here to— Never mind.' She blurted out, 'I've just seen Jo.'

'Seen her?'

'Look, I didn't mean to say that. It's…it's medical and confidential and between me and Jo.'

Jo, who had opened her office door a bare three inches and was now leaning heavily on the handle because she wasn't confident her legs would hold her up.

Tell him, Tara. You've just blurted out exactly what you told me you *didn't* want Rip to know, so finish the job.

Ask him to meet you in the café so you can tell him, because this *has* to come out in the open, and I can't hang in limbo much longer the way I have been.

But Tara didn't say anything more, and a few seconds later the street door opened and closed. She'd gone.

When Jo marshalled enough impetus to leave her office, Rip was still in the waiting room, looking at his ex-wife's hurried progress down the front steps and along the street. He saw Jo at once—for the first time that morning, as it happened. Their comings and goings hadn't managed to co-ordinate until now.

He must have read something in her face, because he frowned and stepped closer. 'You all right?'

'Going home for lunch. Tense morning, and I need a break.'

'Need a lunch partner?'

She didn't. Not if it was Rip. Not now. 'Time to myself, I think.'

He looked concerned, but didn't push. 'Maybe tonight.'

She nodded. Maybe. 'Tara wanted me to tell you—I mean, you saw her just now, but she forgot to say it—that she'd be in the café if you needed to see her.'

'Thanks. OK.'

Do you need to see her?

She didn't ask, just gave a couple of quick instructions to Merril and Trudy and went out the door. As it had been on the weekend, the weather was still bright, and the sky a glorious Vermont blue. She left her car parked at the side of the building and walked, needing the repetitive exercise, the fresh air, the space.

Nina's house came into view almost as soon as she'd set off—a pretty little clapboard place much like her own. She thought about Nina, her courage and warmth, her enthusiasm for the kind of devoted parenthood that wasn't an easy role in combination with her illness, and wished they knew each other better. She was desperate for another woman to talk to.

Could I?

Download some of this?

But how could I tell her how I'm feeling, and tell her about Rip, without bringing Tara's pregnancy into it?

Reaching the house, she stopped outside the front gate, inner debate raging. If there was a way she could talk about everything in generalised language, no names attached, and avoid the subject of Tara…

She didn't realise that Nina had come around the side of the house with Genie until the dog, prancing ahead, had almost reached her. 'Hi, Jo!' Nina said. 'Were you stopping by?'

'I was trying to decide whether to stop by,' Jo answered. 'But I'm on my way home for lunch so it would have been a quick one. And I see you're going out. I won't trouble you for coffee, then.'

'Genie's demanding a walk, and I've been sitting at the computer all morning, so she didn't have to argue too hard. Cody's started his day-care—he's almost forgotten the hospital already—and Alice is in school, so my good girl is bored. I'll let her off the leash for a minute while we talk.'

She bent down, and the dog seized on her new freedom and began to explore some complex scent trail that apparently wound around the sidewalk like a child's scribble pattern. Jo knew that if Genie had sensed an imminent seizure, she would have stayed much more closely by her mistress's side.

Even though it was only a few minutes of small talk, the conversation grounded Jo a little, settled her jumpy nerves.

I'll get through this, she thought. If Rip and Tara do pick up their marriage again, I still have options. If it gets too hard, I can leave Harriet. It wouldn't be an impossible transition and I wouldn't be letting Rip down. We'll have Shelley on board by then.

The new doctor was due to arrive any day, to start settling her little family in before she officially began work next Monday.

'Really nice meal the other night,' Nina was saying. 'Sandy got me inspired to try something crafty.'

A battered old pick-up truck turned into the street, higher up the hill. It had taken the corner a little too fast, Jo registered.

'Yes, inspirational is the word when it comes to Sandy,' she said to Nina. 'Don't ever try telling her you don't have an eye for design. She'll just tell you that you haven't yet tapped into—'

The pick-up was still coming too fast, and it wasn't in the right place on the road. It was going to run up the kerb. The whole thing happened in a second, too fast for any creature to move. The tyre hit the cement with a bone-jarring bump. Nina screamed. Genie was no more than a messy blob of black, right in the shadow of the big vehicle's wheel. Jo heard a high-pitched, horrible yelp and her stomach gave a sickening sideways jolt.

The pick-up lurched away, back onto the road. Its brakes wrenched on and it stopped at an angle, its suspension rocking with the suddenness of its halt. Nina was screaming and running for her dog, who was moving, Jo registered. Moving strangely. Alive, then. Badly injured?

'Genie! Genie! Oh, dear God, Genie! Oh, God, is she hurt?'

'Oh, hell, what have I done? What did I do?'

The driver of the pick-up had jumped from his vehicle, leaving it still in the road, where another car nosed cautiously around it and on up the hill, the young female driver not deeming it necessary to stop.

The man—quite old, thin white hair—ran towards Nina and her dog, cursing himself and almost sobbing. At the kerb, he fell, but sat up at once, writhing and clutching his ankle...and his chest.

And even though it felt wrong, Jo knew that as a doctor she had to choose the human being over the dog.

'Yes, your temperature's very high, Bill, 103 degrees,' Rip told Harry Brown's dad, forcing his concentration.

Don't miss something important, he told himself, just because you're thinking about Jo.

Like hers did, his office faced the street and he'd seen her walking past on her way home for lunch. She hadn't taken her car, which was parked in one of the reserved spaces on the other side of the building.

Bill Brown had booked a double appointment this morning, for his son's continuing daily blood test and check-up and because he himself was sick. Harry's blood tests continued to show an improvement in his platelet count, and Rip had found no evidence of further bleeding in the five-year-old. At the moment, Harry was playing with the toy-box that Rip kept for kids, and you would never have known how recently his life had hung so precariously in the balance.

'But your chest sounds good,' he told Bill. 'It's not pneumonia. It's just a dose of flu.'

Jo must be halfway up the hill by now, passing that pretty little place the Grafton family had just moved into. He so badly wanted to talk to her. He'd gone round to her house last night after Tara's car had taunted him with its innocent presence in the hotel parking lot, but as he'd pulled to the kerb outside her house, he'd seen the last light go off in an upstairs window.

It had been after eleven-thirty. He had decided not to get her out of bed when he had no idea how she'd react to what he'd wanted to say.

'I'm a bit run down, and I've lost weight,' Bill Brown was saying. 'This thing with Harry's platelet count rocked both of us, Vanessa and me.'

'She's not with you today?'

'She had to start work again this morning, down in Rutland. It was great that she managed to get the time off.'

'I was going to suggest she send you to bed for a few days, give you some TLC.'

Bill must have read a few unsaid things in Rip's words. He sighed and stretched his face into a grimace. 'Yeah, things were looking good with us for a while. This scare over Harry reminded us of...well, you know, and I think we both thought for a couple of days... But the problems hadn't really gone away. It's too late for us, we've realised.'

'Yes, you can get to that point, can't you?' Rip said. 'When it's just too late.'

The words sounded ominous in his own ears.

Had he left it too late with Jo?

Timing could count for so much.

'So she's back in Rutland,' Bill went on. His tone was limp and he looked as if every bone in his body ached. 'Harry's a good kid, though. He'll let me lie on the couch all day, and I can send him over to our neighbours for a play later on.'

'Come in again if you feel worse. And drink lots of fluid.'

Turning into her front yard by now maybe, Rip's thoughts ran. Or maybe her legs were still sore from skiing and she'd taken the steeper stretch more slowly.

'Thanks,' Bill said. 'Come on, Harry, let's pack up the toys.'

He bent to help his son finish the job, with a further instruction about not throwing the blocks, but then his words were cut across by a squeal of brakes and the sound of screaming. Rip went still.

Where had those sounds come from?

From Main Street, running parallel to this one?

Or from this street, further up the hill?

He stood up and ushered father and son out of his office,

the mental image of Jo walking up the street, which had been running like a silent movie in the background of his thoughts all through this appointment with the Browns, playing through more vividly than ever. He was sure those sounds had come from up the hill, and he wasn't going to wait any longer to confirm his fear.

If something had happened to her, before they'd had a chance to talk…

Hell, scratch that!

The talk didn't matter.

If something had happened to her, period.

'Lunch-break,' he told Trudy.

'Did you hear that car?' She was on the alert also.

'Yes, I'm going to check it out. Where do you think it was coming from?'

'Main Street?'

'No, I don't think it was. I really don't think it was from Main Street. I think it was coming from up the hill…'

Fear rising, he quickened his pace, car keys already in his hand.

CHAPTER ELEVEN

IT MUST have taken less than a minute for Rip to scream up the hill in his car. Halfway to the scene, he could see that his intuition and his directional hearing had been correct. This was where the squeal of brakes had come from.

He jammed the car against the kerb, slammed on the brakes, and jumped out, taking in what he saw.

Jo was there, but she wasn't hurt.

First critical piece of information, and a sight that sent such a powerful wave of relief over him that it threatened to knock him to the ground.

'Jo!' His voice cracked as he said her name, and cracked harder when he swore. 'I knew you'd walked up. I was thinking about you. And then I heard the brakes and the screams.' He couldn't go on.

'No, it wasn't me.' She sounded as shaky as he felt, and her eyes were huge as she fixed them on his face. 'It's OK, Rip. It wasn't me.'

'Thank God!' It was a prayer more than an exclamation.

He mastered himself and began to think like a doctor, not like a man. Giving a steady stream of reassurance, she was bending over a form that looked familiar—the weight, the style of clothing, the white hair.

Thornton Liddle. It was his pick-up, still parked askew in the middle of the road.

His squealing brakes, too, Rip guessed. He saw the dog and Nina Grafton, bent like Jo over the animal, but frantically sobbing. 'I think she's OK. Oh, darling Genie, are you OK? You're breathing, but why are you lying down? Genie, show me if you're hurt, princess…'

'I'll take a look at her for you as soon as I can,' Rip told Nina. Then added, 'Jo? Is it his heart?'

He didn't want to have to deal with this. All he wanted to do was to sweep Jo up in his arms and tell her over and over how glad he was—'glad' was way too weak a word!— that she was all right. But he couldn't let her see that now, couldn't let other people down when he was needed.

'I'm not sure yet.' Jo was trying to help the old man as he struggled to pull himself into a sitting position, as if clawing his way to the surface of a swimming pool in search of air. 'Not getting a verbal response.' She turned at once back to her patient. 'Mr Liddle, you're OK. You've got two doctors here now, and we're going to take care of you.'

Thornton was gasping and groaning, his face beaded with sweat. It could easily be his heart. 'Is the dog…OK?' he managed to say at last.

'She's alive,' Rip answered.

'I shouldn't still be driving. You've tried to tell me that. And Mona. I lost control on the bend, just couldn't seem to see the road.' He stopped for breath, and Jo began to loosen his clothing. His colour looked a little better.

'Never mind what happened, Thornton, tell us about the pain,' Rip said.

'I can't get my breath.'

'Try to calm down. We're here and you're fine.'

'The pick-up…'

'Give me the keys and I'll move it. It's not safe there, is it?'

'No.'

'But first, please, are you in pain?'

Jo was taking his pulse. She looked up at Rip and

mouthed, 'Strong and steady.' Which was better than they'd both feared. Her eyes still held that wide, questioning look that Rip couldn't answer. Not here. Not now.

But later, yes, if he had to move mountains, he was going to get her alone and they were going to talk.

'Winded myself when I fell. Pulled a shoulder muscle, I think.' Thornton said. He rubbed at it, then added, 'Yeah.'

Jo and Rip looked at each other again. His voice sounded stronger. He didn't look grey. He wasn't in the grip of a full-on heart attack's inexorable agony, but they couldn't be sure yet that he was safe. His hands were trembling.

'He tripped on the kerb,' Jo said.

'So you saw the accident itself?'

'Yes, Nina and I were standing right here. Can you move your ankle, Mr Liddle? You were grabbing it before, and I'm wondering if it's sprained. I think we should get you into Rip's car and get you down to the practice, but I'm not sure how well you can walk.'

Rip moved the pick-up to a safe position, then returned to help Jo and the old man as he managed to stand. 'I think I'm OK,' he gasped, once on his feet. 'It was the shock. The dog...'

Genie was standing now, too, with Nina still hugging her close, looking into her doggy eyes, feeling her body for signs of injury.

'She definitely got knocked,' Nina said. 'Please, can we check her now? I know she's only a dog...' She had tears coursing down her cheeks.

'Jo? While I help Mr Liddle into the car?' Rip said. 'Nina, we know she's not just a dog.'

'Yes, if you can manage,' Jo said, in answer to Rip's question.

'We can.' He helped his patient into the passenger seat and went to climb in the other side.

'Not going yet. I want to hear the news on the dog,' Thornton Liddle said. 'And I want a cigarette.' He was already patting at his pocket.

Rip thought about trying to stop him, but then gave a mental shrug. He realised that he hadn't even thought about a cigarette himself since he'd heard the squeal of brakes—or even, come to think of it, last night when Tara had used her scare tactics on him.

He felt his spirits rising, although he knew it was really too soon for that. He had a lot to say to Jo, in stronger and more unequivocal language, even, than he would have used to her twelve hours ago. And he knew he couldn't count on her answer. Not after what he'd put her through lately.

'We should run her to the vet just to check,' Jo was saying when Rip walked back to the patch of grass where she and Nina both hovered over the dog. 'But I can't find any obvious breaks, or any blood. Her pupils look normal, she's standing up steadily now.'

'And wagging her tail,' Nina said. 'Oh, Genie!'

'She might just have got winded and shocked, too, but let's get her checked out properly. I'll have to go down and bring up my car.'

'I'll wait here with her,' Nina said.

'And I'll drive you down, Jo,' Rip came in.

'I'm going to hand in my licence,' Thornton Liddle announced in the car. His hands were still shaking, Rip saw. 'Mona can play chauffeur. Let's face it, I'm never going to get free of the cigarettes, but this I can do. Flipping heck, if I'd killed or maimed that dog, that nice woman's pet!'

'More than that, Thornton,' Rip told him, and sketched for the old man just how important Genie was in Nina Grafton's life.

Mr Liddle groaned. 'So if I'd killed her...'

At the surgery, Rip took the old man's blood pressure,

temperature and pulse, and listened to his breathing. The blood-pressure reading was too high, the ankle was definitely sprained, possibly fractured, and he had localised tenderness above his collar-bone also. Although the signs didn't point to a major heart problem, Rip decided to play it safe, call an ambulance and get him admitted for overnight observation.

They were still waiting for the ambulance when Jo returned from driving Nina and Genie to the vet. Rip stood in the waiting room, talking to Trudy and Merril, and her attention went instinctively to him. Nobody else mattered. She'd seen the way he'd looked at her outside the Graftons' house when he'd first seen that she was there at the scene of the near-accident but that she was safe.

'Nina's husband is going to pick them up and take them home,' she reported. 'I didn't stay, but Genie was practically talking to Nina, saying she was OK. Nina's starting to believe her.' She smiled at Rip, and he smiled back.

Two people came up the front steps. They couldn't be the ambulance paramedics because they weren't wearing uniforms, and anyhow there was no big white vehicle parked out front.

Oh, and in addition they had a baby!

'Shelley!' Rip said, at the same moment that Jo, Trudy and Merril recognised the new arrivals. 'Weren't you getting here tomorrow?'

'Lloyd's sister took Hayley all weekend. We were ready to go by bedtime last night, and then she woke up at, would you believe, four this morning, didn't you, sweetheart?'

'You weren't calling her ''sweetheart'' at that hour,' Lloyd Breck came in, as he gave Rip's hand a hearty shake. 'I think the words ''spawn'' and ''devil'' were mentioned.'

'You know I was over that in five minutes! But, yes, so

we decided we may as well just get on the road.' She grinned.

Since it wasn't currently four in the morning, Jo felt no ambivalence about the baby. Hayley was adorable. Dressed in a little peach-coloured playsuit with a hat to match, she sat happily in Shelley's arms, facing the world and smiling at everything she saw.

'May I have a hold?' Jo asked.

She still felt shaky. About Thornton Liddle. About Genie. About Tara's visit that morning. About Rip. About everything. A baby was just what she needed as she couldn't talk to Rip in private right now.

A patient arrived. Rip's. His lunch-break was over, but hers needn't be just yet. She still had time for a little bit of baby-hugging. No time to eat, but her stomach felt too churned up for that anyhow.

'Of course you can have a hold,' Shelley said.

Jo coaxed a couple of gorgeous coos and smiles from Hayley, then heard the ambulance pull up noisily outside. Rip hadn't called his patient in yet. He opened the door, watching the paramedics as they unloaded the stretcher that would take Thornton Liddle into the back of the vehicle. But when the next set of feet sounded on the steps they didn't belong to the paramedics.

Tara. Not in a mood to waste any more time. 'Look, Rip, I'm not going to mess around any more. I've been sitting in that café and you didn't come! I need to see you. Do you know why? Jo, did you tell him?'

'No, Tara,' Jo answered. 'I told you I wouldn't, and I didn't.' She handed Hayley back to Shelley, who kissed the fat little cheeks then passed the baby on to Lloyd.

Tara made an impatient, disgusted sound. 'You *didn't*? You really can't take a hint, can you?'

Several puzzle pieces dropped into place in Jo's mind

with a brittle click. '*That's* why you came to see me? Because you *wanted* me to tell—?'

'It doesn't matter now,' Tara said, while Jo's brain went on ticking and clicking.

Tara had known perfectly well she was pregnant—had known before she'd ever come back to Vermont, had known she wasn't just at four or five weeks, and had taken advantage of a tiny smear of bleeding to manufacture a miscarriage scare in order to try a second time to con Jo into giving Rip the news, using the upside-down tactic of begging her for secrecy because she'd wanted Rip's help but hadn't wanted to have to ask for it.

'It was stupid,' Tara declared.

Worse than stupid, Jo considered. She'd witnessed Tara's use of this kind of tactic before, during the marriage, but it had been over trivial issues not something like this.

'Rip?' His ex-wife made a beseeching face.

'I can't talk to you now, Tara.' He sounded as angry as Jo felt on his behalf. 'Jo, I have a patient waiting, but if I didn't, if there's anyone I want to talk to, it's you.'

'No,' she told him firmly. 'You need to talk to Tara.'

'When you've seen me, Rip,' Tara came in, 'you may not need to see Jo. I didn't want it to happen like this. I've probably handled the whole thing wrong. I have. I've been stupid about it. But I didn't know what else to do. Rip, I'm scared. No more games, I promise, just the truth, and I really need to see you in private now.'

'Jo?' Rip said.

'See her,' she told him again. 'I'll—I'll juggle your appointments somehow.'

Through all this, Shelley had stayed silent, but now she spoke. 'Let me juggle them, too. I can get a head start. As long as Lloyd takes Hayley and someone—anyone!—gets me a coffee!'

'Honey?' Lloyd said. 'You're sure?'

'Call it a trial run before next Monday. Hayley needs a play in the park on the baby swings. And a few things clearly need to get settled between a few people here. Jo, we'll go into your office and you can fill me in. Everything I need to know in three sentences. Trudy will trouble-shoot for me on admin procedure. Give me the easy patients. Your office, right?'

She went in the right direction, and Jo followed. They both arrived in good time to see Rip and Tara going past the window at the front of the office, and to hear quite clearly when Tara told Rip, 'I'm pregnant.'

Shelley blew out a breath. 'I guess we're not up to the three sentences on the practice yet,' she said. 'Sounds like I need the three sentences on our senior partner's personal life first.'

'Oh, lord, there's nothing I'd like more than to talk about it!' Jo answered, practically in tears. 'She first came to me about her pregnancy last week, and I haven't been able to say a thing.'

She launched into the story. She didn't intend admitting, at first, to how personally involved she felt—that horrible sense of competition, the backdating of her feelings for Rip which made it seem, suddenly, as if this had all been going on for years. But then it just came out in a chaotic gush that Shelley frowned at, struggling to follow as she drank the coffee Trudy had brought her.

'So the baby's not his?'

'No.'

'But the other relationship, the one she left Rip for, that's broken up and she's looking for a substitute father.'

'I think so. I doubt she'd ever put it so bluntly. She's—'

'A manipulator. That was clear.'

'Rip's always known it, too. He's not been blind, just

very ready to forgive.' Jo considered telling Shelley about Rip's mother and her serial divorces, but Shelley didn't need that level of detail right now.

'Our niece tried the same thing,' the new partner said. 'Looking for a substitute father, I mean, before she made the decision to give Hayley to us.'

'It must be a difficult position to be in.'

Shelley snorted. 'For Michaela, yes. She was just sixteen and, well, a darling but clueless, no idea about a career, with parents who aren't by any means well off. I don't consider it's a difficult position for Tara, though. She's how old?'

'Around thirty-four.'

'Good career?'

'Trust fund. Modest, apparently, but enough to live on. And she'll make some money from her quilts if she works at it.'

Shelley snorted again. 'Forget the quilts! Jo, she has options, talents and enough brains, experience and resources to work out which of those options she wants to take. I am going to go to the park to meet Lloyd and Hayley in a little while, when Rip gets back, and I am going to hug Hayley and hold her to my heart, and I am *not* going to feel sorry for Rip's ex-wife!'

It was the best thing she could have said, and it freed Jo from any sense of emotional responsibility for Tara, even though it couldn't free her from her stomach-caving fear that this was all too messy and hard and that even if Tara left Harriet, even if Rip sent her away, it didn't mean that he cared about Jo the way Jo needed him to, ached for him to.

The waiting room was filling fast, and Tara and Rip weren't yet back, so Jo and Shelley did the only thing they could do. They saw patients, with Shelley working in Rip's office and directing questions to Trudy or Merril whenever she needed to.

At some point, suddenly, Jo realised that it wasn't Shelley seeing Rip's patients any more, it was Rip himself, and that Shelley must have gone to meet Lloyd and the baby. But the clock only said a quarter after two, so she had almost another four hours of this—of hearing his voice, glimpsing him, not being able to talk.

Finally, at ten after six, they were done.

'I'll lock,' Trudy said, in a grim, don't-you-dare-argue kind of voice.

Argue?

It was the last thing Jo wanted to do.

'Are we going to talk?' she asked Rip.

'Try suggesting anything else and see where it gets you.'

'Go!' Trudy pushed them out the door. 'Rip, when you came out of your office after we heard those brakes squealing over lunch and I saw your face when you thought it might be Jo...' She lifted her hands. 'Do this right!'

Shelley's direct manner seemed to be catching.

'Intending to, Trudy. Let's walk,' Rip said to Jo, dropping his voice. His brown eyes held a smoky, suffering look in their depths. 'I couldn't sit in that café again. I need some air.'

'Where is she? Tara,' Jo corrected herself. She hated the *she,* the Other Woman *she* that should be spelled with a capital letter also. 'Where's Tara?'

'Checked out of her hotel and on the road by now, I should think.' Rip touched Jo's back lightly as she went down the steps ahead of him. 'And I hope!'

'To where?'

'I didn't ask. Her parents in Boston maybe. She has options.'

'That's what Shelley said.'

'You told her about all this?' He paused in his stride. They were just about to cross the road, heading for the street that led up the hill past Nina's place.

'I offloaded a bit, yes.'

'What did you say? No, forget what you said. You had every right to offload.' He began to walk again. 'Let me talk, first. Jo, this has been impossible. It might still be impossible.'

'To be a father to someone else's child?'

'You think that's why I sent her away? Because I didn't want to step in and take on Serrano's baby? No! I didn't need to hear about her pregnancy to understand my own heart. I'd already realised that there was no chance for Tara and me. It hit me like a ton of bricks last night when I left a message on her— That's not important.'

'No?' she said mildly.

'OK.' He gave a short nod. 'I owe you the detail, don't I?'

'Think so, Rip.'

'I left a message on her voicemail asking her to call me back, and she didn't because she wanted to give me a scare. And I'd forgiven that sort of thing from her so many times before and suddenly it was more than something to forgive about her, it was something I just—didn't—*like*—about her, more than just a quirk, the whole package, way too indicative of who she was at heart. I didn't even want there to be a chance for Tara and me any more. I wouldn't have taken that chance if it had been handed to me on a plate, with every promise under the sun from Tara about how she'd changed and what she'd do differently. That was the big change in my thinking, and it unlocked everything else. The only chance I want is with you.'

'Oh, Rip…'

'There's a whole lot more to say but the bottom line is

I love you, and if I hadn't been so stubborn about not repeating my mother's serial mistakes, I might have realised it long ago.'

'Long ago?' She squeezed his arm. 'You first kissed me last week.'

'Hey, please! The week before last.'

He kissed her again now, and she laughed because who kissed a woman on her eyebrow? They had to stop so he could find some better places, which didn't take him long. Actually kissing those places took longer. The light began to fade.

'I loved you before I kissed you, Jo,' he whispered. 'We were both just too distracted to notice.'

'You think so?'

They kept walking.

'Both too comfortable with each other, and it all changed in our hearts too gradually, until—'

'Until the day you quit smoking.'

'Don't you feel as if it's been forever? Forever in a good—the best—the very best way. I can't remember when I didn't feel like this.'

She laughed. 'Yes. You too? I've been backdating you, like a dodgy patient history. You know…' She parodied her own professional manner. 'When did you first notice these alarming symptoms, Mrs X.?'

'When did you first notice these alarming symptoms, Dr Middleton?'

'The wanting-to-kiss-you symptoms?'

'Those, and can I ask? Are there any others?'

'Oh, lots! They're all fabulous, but I can't begin to describe them.'

'Marry me, and we'll have plenty of time.'

'Marry you?' Even now, with him looking at her like this, eyes ablaze, in the middle of a Harriet, Vermont sidewalk late on a Monday afternoon, Jo hadn't expected it, not so soon.

He saw it in her face. 'Didn't you think I was sure? Are you not sure yourself?'

'Oh, Rip! Yes, I'm sure.'

'So am I…'

And those were both statements that bore repeating several times just to be on the safe side. They reached her house, but weren't ready to stop walking just yet. Still laughing and crying, Jo saw something on the porch, through the tears in her eyes, and went to check.

'Look, someone's sent you flowers,' Rip said lightly.

'Who, I wonder?' she murmured, bending to pick up the card.

'Me, actually.'

'They're beautiful!'

'Leave them. They'll keep. Let's keep walking.'

'Tell me why you're so sure, Rip.'

'That we should keep walking?'

'Sure about us. You knew that's what I meant. But the walking is nice, too.'

'Why I'm so sure? Because of how I feel. Because it's you. Because of who you are. Because this time it won't be me doing all the work, determined to do the work because if I don't do it—if *I* don't do it, because noone else is going to—that'll mean failure. It took me way too long to realise a marriage couldn't work that way—too much of a reaction against the effort my mother never managed to put in. The commitment and the effort can't be all on one side.'

'At the moment, it doesn't feel like a huge effort, I have to say,' Jo murmured.

'But you know, Jo. You know about the commitment, and the effort. When you agreed to go skiing, even though

I'd given you no reason to think we'd have a good day, you took a deep breath and did it. You didn't throw a tantrum and demand to be taken home. You know about the courage and the trust. Tara never did. She only knew about the games and the self-interest.'

'There was more to your marriage than that, Rip. You would never have married her in the first place if there hadn't been.' Jo felt able to say this now, with his arm around her, his head leaning down to her shoulder, all the evidence that he just couldn't let her go and didn't want to.

'Oh, of course there was. In the beginning, anyhow. She always used to remind me of my favourite cousin Lena, I think that was part of it. Lena was a year older than I was, and I was an only child, so I was lonely sometimes. Her visits always had an aura of mischief and magic. We had these crazy adventures, and I forgave the way she teased me because of that. And I think I saw a lot of—' He stopped. 'Why are we still talking about Tara?'

'We're not.' Jo hugged him. 'We're talking about Lena. Much more interesting. I'll look forward to meeting her.'

'I want to talk about us.' He tightened the hug, nuzzled her neck.

'That's a pretty interesting subject, too...'

They covered a lot of ground in a very short space of time—practical details at first, such as which house they would live in. Hers, they decided. His they would offer for sale or rent to Shelley and Lloyd, because of the option of building a studio-cum-office at the back for Lloyd to work in.

Then the details became less practical...

The honeymoon destination was a contentious issue. Jo wanted Paris, and Rip wanted the Caribbean. They talked about a compromise, then they decided they'd go for both.

Paris late in the spring, after a wedding they didn't want to wait long for or make too elaborate, and the Caribbean next winter, because even though Vermont was a very good showcase for cold things, a hot sandy beach had its attractions, too.

That cute baby Hayley had put a few ideas into Jo's head, and Rip seized on the ideas with such enthusiasm that Jo suspected she had a good shot at being pregnant by the end of the day.

They reached Rip's house.

'You have flowers on your porch, too,' Jo said.

'Also sent by me.'

'You sent yourself flowers?'

'No, I sent you flowers, more flowers, because I hoped we might end up either at your place or mine, but I didn't know which it would be—I didn't realise we'd walk past both—and I really wanted you to have flowers, because it was easier to organise over the phone than, oh, the moon and stars.'

'You want me to have those?'

'There are so many things I want you to have, Jo, I don't even know where to start.' He turned her into his arms, ready to kiss her again.

'So you started with flowers?' she whispered.

'Five years in partnership, and we're still just at the start of everything. Don't you think that's great?' he whispered back.

She did.

EPILOGUE

RIP and Jo had a three-tiered, three-flavoured Vermont ice-cream cake for their spring wedding. They had rain in Paris for their honeymoon, along with chocolate croissants and art museums and window-shopping under a big umbrella, and a whole lot of other things which meant the rain didn't matter at all. By December, on the follow-up honeymoon in the Caribbean, they got sunshine, and they were back to ice cream.

Cravings for ice cream, to be specific.

Midnight cravings for strawberry and coffee and something with nuts in it, satisfied only by a desperate last-minute call to room service before it ceased operation for the night.

'I'm sorry, Rip,' Jo said. 'You're probably dying to get to sleep.'

'I'm not dying to get to sleep,' he answered.

'How can they tell you it's going to take forty-five minutes to deliver ice cream? I hope that's forty-five minutes *before* it gets scooped out, not forty-five minutes melting in a bowl on the way from the kitchens.'

'I'm not sorry at all.'

'No?'

'It's another incentive for us to stay awake.'

'What's the first incent— Oh!' She grinned and her eyes lit up, which gave him a wash of relief because he'd wondered if he was being a little optimistic on that front at this hour of the night.

Jo was three and a half months pregnant—beyond the

nausea and crippling fatigue she'd experienced over the past couple of months and into the hungry stage, but a little unpredictable when it came to certain other appetites.

Since Rip currently considered her to be the most beautiful example of the female form he'd ever seen in his life, with her ripening breasts, lustrous hair and newly rounded stomach, his own appetite was pitched at a steady 'off the chart' and he suffered from the unpredictability at times.

Suffer? He didn't suffer! Not in any serious sense. Their marriage was glorious.

He'd received a birth announcement from Tara back in September, the same day that Jo had taken her positive pregnancy test. Tara had had a baby girl. He was happy for her, and he hadn't given the news more than three minutes' worth of thought since. The baby wasn't his, and Tara just wasn't important any more.

This was important.

Jo was important.

'I don't think we'd better count on the whole forty-five minutes,' she said seriously. 'Last night, with the banana split with almonds and hot fudge, they said twenty, and they were quicker.'

'So we're trying for a speed record?'

'Think so.'

'Does that mean I don't have time to watch you undress?'

'I'll undress fast.'

'Not so it's a blur, Jo, because I like—'

She grinned again. 'I know what you like…'

She did. That was the great thing about her. She knew what he liked, and she wanted to give it to him—the meals he liked, the conversation he liked, the particular way of removing that little, snug-fitting, blue cotton knit, vest-style pyjama top that he really, really liked and would have to say goodbye to soon until after the pregnancy.

No strings attached with any of the giving. No return favours expected later. No leverage, or pay-back, or manipulation hidden beneath.

He was the luckiest man in the world, and he planned to spend the rest of his life valuing the luck and sharing it with Jo. No games this time around. Only sharing and generosity instead. Sharing the good and the bad, just as they'd promised during their simple wedding ceremony.

Now, with their hotel room window open to let in a milky Caribbean night, they shared twenty-seven minutes of love-making—not really a speed record, by the way—and when the ice cream arrived three minutes later, they shared that, too.

'I'm very, very happy, Jo,' Rip told his wife.

'So am I,' she whispered back, then she kissed away the taste of strawberry from his lips.

MILLS & BOON

Medical romance™

presents an exciting and emotional new trilogy from bestselling author Kate Hardy

Posh Docs!

HONOURABLE, ELIGIBLE AND IN DEMAND!

Her Celebrity Surgeon

On sale 6th January 2006

Don't miss the next two novels
Her Honourable Playboy *(on sale 3rd March 2006)*
His Honourable Surgeon *(on sale 5th May 2006)*
– only from Medical Romance!

Available at most branches of WHSmith, Tesco, ASDA, Borders, Eason, Sainsbury's and most bookshops

Visit our website at www.millsandboon.co.uk

MILLS & BOON®

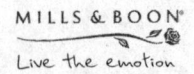

Live the emotion

Medical
romance™

HER CELEBRITY SURGEON by *Kate Hardy*

Fiery registrar Sophie Harrison is furious! She is convinced that the new Director of Surgery has only been appointed for his title. Baron Rupert Charles Radley is a man never out of the gossip rags – but Sophie soon learns that beneath the title is a genuine, caring man…

POSH DOCS: Honourable, eligible, and in demand!

COMING BACK FOR HIS BRIDE
by *Abigail Gordon*

As a teenager Isabel West was devastated when young GP Ross Templeton suddenly left the village. Now, he's back – and he's her boss! Isabel is determined not to risk her heart again. But Ross never wanted to leave her…and he's come back to prove his love…!

A PERFECT FATHER by *Laura Iding*

Moriah fell in love with Blake in the heat of a Peruvian mission. But after one passionate night he broke her heart. Now she'll be working with him again! Blake hasn't been able to forget Moriah, but he must resist the attraction he feels – he can *never* be the perfect father she's looking for. But Moriah is determined to convince him that he's wrong.

On sale 6th January 2006

Available at most branches of WHSmith, Tesco, ASDA, Borders, Eason, Sainsbury's and most bookshops

Visit www.millsandboon.co.uk

MILLS & BOON®

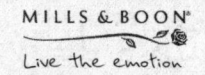

Live the emotion

Medical
romance™

THE NURSE'S SECRET SON by Amy Andrews

Nurse Sophie Monday is the mother of a small boy – a boy everyone believes to be her late husband Michael's. But once she loved his brother Daniel, and when tragedy struck he rejected her, unaware she was carrying his baby. Now Daniel's back – and Sophie must admit the truth!

A&E DRAMA: Pulses are racing in these fast-paced dramatic stories

THE SURGEON'S RESCUE MISSION
by Dianne Drake

Solaina saved Dr David Gentry's life when she found him injured in the jungle. As she nursed him back to health he nurtured feelings in her she'd never known. But soon they find themselves in a dangerous situation that could cost them their lives – and the lives of their patients!

24:7 Feel the heat – every hour...every minute... every heartbeat

THE PREGNANT GP by Judy Campbell

Lisa Balfour has come to Arrandale to be the town's GP. She soon finds herself attracted to gorgeous doctor Ronan Gillespie – but one night of passion results in her pregnancy, and she's faced with a heart-wrenching dilemma. She must keep her pregnancy a secret...

On sale 6th January 2006

Available at most branches of WHSmith, Tesco, ASDA, Borders, Eason, Sainsbury's and most bookshops

Visit www.millsandboon.co.uk

When baby's delivered just in time for Christmas!

This Christmas, three loving couples receive the most precious gift of all!

Don't miss out on *Precious Gifts* on sale 2nd December 2005

Available at most branches of WHSmith, Tesco, ASDA, Borders, Eason, Sainsbury's and most bookshops

www.millsandboon.co.uk

*More life, love and family
for your money!*

SPECIAL EDITION™

Extra

Author of over ninety-five books and two-time RWA RITA® Award finalist

JOAN ELLIOTT PICKART

**presents a new novel
featuring an unknown MacAllister**

MacAllister's Return

When DA Jesse Burke discovers that his parents stole him from his real family, he needs to at least see his twin and his biological mother and father. Then he finds himself with a beautiful mediator, determined to nurture him!

*Available at most branches of WHSmith, Tesco, ASDA,
Borders, Eason, Sainsbury's and most bookshops*

www.silhouette.co.uk

FREE!

4 Books
and a surprise gift!

We would like to take this opportunity to thank you for reading this Mills & Boon® book by offering you the chance to take FOUR more specially selected titles from the Medical Romance™ series absolutely FREE! We're also making this offer to introduce you to the benefits of the Reader Service™—

- ★ FREE home delivery
- ★ FREE gifts and competitions
- ★ FREE monthly Newsletter
- ★ Exclusive Reader Service offers
- ★ Books available before they're in the shops

Accepting these FREE books and gift places you under no obligation to buy, you may cancel at any time, even after receiving your free shipment. Simply complete your details below and return the entire page to the address below. You don't even need a stamp!

YES! Please send me 4 free Medical Romance books and a surprise gift. I understand that unless you hear from me, I will receive 6 superb new titles every month for just £2.75 each, postage and packing free. I am under no obligation to purchase any books and may cancel my subscription at any time. The free books and gift will be mine to keep in any case.

M5ZEF

Ms/Mrs/Miss/Mr .... Initials ....
BLOCK CAPITALS PLEASE
Surname ....
Address ....

.........................Postcode ....

Send this whole page to:
UK: FREEPOST CN81, Croydon, CR9 3WZ

Offer valid in UK only and is not available to current Reader service subscribers to this series. Overseas and Eire please write for details. We reserve the right to refuse an application and applicants must be aged 18 years or over. Only one application per household. Terms and prices subject to change without notice. Offer expires 31st March 2006. As a result of this application, you may receive offers from Harlequin Mills & Boon and other carefully selected companies. If you would prefer not to share in this opportunity please write to The Data Manager, PO Box 676, Richmond, TW9 IWU.

Mills & Boon® is a registered trademark owned by Harlequin Mills & Boon Limited.
Medical Romance™ is being used as a trademark. The Reader Service™ is being used as a trademark.